D1745491

Praise for Tilly Greene's *Zandia*

5 Lips and 2 Chilis   "I am never disappointed by Tilly Greene's books, and Zandia is no exception. It's fast paced, and full of sizzling hot sex that will leave you breathless. I could totally feel Sui's need to live her own life. And Xer, who wouldn't want a man like that? He is strong when he needs to be and he knows how to be soft. This is definitely a page turner. Oh and you'll need your own fan."

   ~ *Julianne, TwoLips Reviews*

4.5 Blue Ribbons   "Zandia is a very interesting planet and Greene's story is wonderfully threaded together. Reading it, I really cared about the characters--Sui and Xer as well as the secondary characters.   Tilly Greene has created a whole new world facing a sexual revolution and shows us that even alien feminists can enjoy their sexuality to the fullest!"

   ~ *Chris, Romance Junkies*

4.5 Lips   "ZANDIA keeps the tension high, passion simmering on boil and delivers a kick ass story to the reader! Ms. Greene delivers a fine story that has the reader rooting for Sui to deliver Xei a set down that will shake him to his core yet you can feel the sparks between them. It was a delightful mix in ZANDIA."

   ~ *Dawn, Love Romances and More*

5 Stars/O Heat "Zandia is a superb story that explores the complex emotions between Sui and Xer. Once I started Zandia I became so engrossed in the story, I could not put it down. Bravo Ms. Greene. I can't recommend this book enough. Zandia is the perfect blend of story, red hot sex, and sci-fi elements."

~ *Claudia, Just Erotic Romance Reviews*

Zandia

Tilly Greene

A Samhain Publishing, Ltd. publication.

Samhain Publishing, Ltd.
577 Mulberry Street, Suite 1520
Macon, GA 31201
www.samhainpublishing.com

Zandia
Copyright © 2008 by Tilly Greene
Print ISBN: 1-59998-799-6
Digital ISBN: 1-59998-533-0

Editing by Jessica Bimberg
Cover by Dawn Seewer

This book is a work of fiction. The names, characters, places, and incidents are products of the writer's imagination or have been used fictitiously and are not to be construed as real. Any resemblance to persons, living or dead, actual events, locale or organizations is entirely coincidental.

All Rights Are Reserved. No part of this book may be used or reproduced in any manner whatsoever without written permission, except in the case of brief quotations embodied in critical articles and reviews.

First Samhain Publishing, Ltd. electronic publication: July 2007
First Samhain Publishing, Ltd. print publication: March 2008

Dedication

For Mom—thank you for giving us such a strong sense of self, confidence, and an abundance of love to share. Love you!

Prologue

Her heart pounded fast and hard as she rested her head back against a cold wall in a dark closet.

Sui tried to calm herself by thinking why she was hiding in a guest room closet, located deep in the bowels of her father's official transporter. A lone woman running away from home, much less slipping off to a foreign planet to live and work by herself, was not done. At least she knew of none who had.

But she was desperate, and everyone knows times of desperation are often followed by extreme action.

A few weeks shy of completing instruction for being thrust into the emotive pathline, she'd made this drastic move to change her course. Hopefully it was the right direction. There was no way she could stay on Zandia and remain a healthy and sane woman as an emotionally supportive member for her clan, her extended family. Maybe she was more suited to the traditional roles, she didn't think so, but it was possible. Who knew what they wanted to do at seventeen, other than go out and seek life.

In her case, she'd decided to make her way to another planet to find different options. She wanted to experience life, see the Universe, meet and interact with people outside of her clan. Unfortunately none of this would've been open to her if she'd been sent back home from the National Education Institute having finished the emotive pathline plan.

She held her breath. The footsteps seemed closer now; she could hear them walking around in the hallway outside the room she was hiding in. Darn it! Supposedly no one ever came down here so she shouldn't have had to worry about being found. But here they were, obviously searching for someone or something. If she were located and identified, Sui was positive her father would send her back home to follow her predetermined pathline. The one she didn't believe would ever make her happy.

The voices moved closer and were now in the room itself, but still muffled. There was one voice she could hear in particular, she was sure it was her father's. There were others speaking as well, but she couldn't decipher what they were all saying. Tightening her arms around her legs, she put her chin on her knees and let her breath out as quietly as she could before taking another unsteady gulp in.

For almost two full days she'd hidden on the transporter without a problem, although she was starved because she'd yet to venture out of this room for food. She'd been so confident no one would come down here she'd even used the bed.

In the blink of an eye, she was found, exposed, and yet not entirely. The panel slid open and she looked up into the gaze of her father. He said nothing for a long minute before he closed her inside. In the still air of the closet, she heard him tell everyone to leave the room, stating he'd handle the situation.

The silence was deafening, and yet she still didn't dare move. Maybe in her hunger for sustenance, she'd imagined he'd found her hiding in a closet.

"Young lady, come out of there right now and tell me what's going on."

Unluckily, the voice coming through to her sounded exactly like her father. Foolishly she continued to hold tightly to the hope it was all a delusion. It didn't take long before the panel slid open again, revealing her very real and angry father. All chance of this being a dream was immediately dashed.

"What's going on? Why are you hiding on my transporter?"

"Well, ummm, you see, my time at the NEI was almost at an end and, well—"

"Sui!"

In the face of her parent's displeasure, a remarkable calm bloomed through her. Propelling the feeling was the understanding this was a chance to plead her case. It had to be taken, otherwise she may end up right back where she'd been. She stood, straight and tall, stepped out of the closet and forward, meeting him on equal footing. With all the respect due him as an adult and her father, she spoke her piece.

"I believe the pathline chosen for me to follow is not the one I'm best suited to live. In fact I'm not sure which one I'd fit well within if given a choice. It's clear to me I'm not an entirely emotionally supportive person, although I do feel for others and wish to love and comfort them, ensure they are happy in their lives. But did you know all through school I was close to failing my emotive courses? It's true, and yet at the same time, I'm not a perfect fit for the traditional sexual-based paths either. The role of a mate, companion, and especially the sexual aide, are demeaning to my intelligence and I know I'm worth more than the use of my body.

"To be honest, Father, I have problems with all the paths offered to females and can't possibly be the only person who has this difficulty. Did you know there is no help for those of us who don't fit into the box society has laid out? I can't tell you how many times I asked my counselor at NEI about my problem, asked for guidance and each time was told the pathline assigned by the leaders was the only one open to me. I was left in the dark to flounder for a sense of self and meanwhile was instructed to quietly accept a life that didn't remotely suit me."

She paused for a brief moment, catching her breath before continuing with her explanation.

"I'm sure you've noticed throughout Zandia, women hold no positions of substance, not in the military, cross-Universe or business areas, and yet we have brains and ideas too. We're given no respect, and if we are seen at all, it's merely as objects of lust, existing to slake man's desire upon or procreate. It is not a fulfilling life."

"I didn't realize you were this unhappy."

His words encouraged her to go on and tell him of the decision she'd made.

"Father, I know I can be a productive person, offer something to society, only not on Zandia. There I'm nothing and can't even be responsible for myself, someone who doesn't know me sets my future. They read test results from my childhood and decide if I'm better suited to be a mate, companion, sexual aide or the woman who offers emotional comforts to her clan, and never should the lines be blurred."

After the words and jumbled thoughts had finally been pulled together and spoken aloud, she felt freer than when she'd snuck on board his transporter. She'd believed running away had been the best solution, but in the end it had been telling someone, especially her father, about the turmoil she'd lived with for years. Surprisingly, it didn't bother her that the declaration was met with a long and drawn out silence, not when it was obvious to her he'd taken in everything she had to say. It was something, every little bit counted because it would've killed her to have her problems dismissed without thought.

"It seems we have much to talk about."

"You aren't going to send me back, are you?"

"I haven't decided, but I'll give you time to convince me of your position."

"Thank you, Father."

"Now, what are we going to do about your being here on my transporter? It isn't safe..."

"I'm fine, I've been chipped and my virus bank was updated before I left. I also still have an infertility device implanted."

"Sui!"

"What? All I'm saying is I can go anywhere in the Universe you can go. You do realize I'm already seventeen years, almost eighteen, and I'm not stupid."

"Well, for now it'd be best if no one knew you, my daughter, were here."

"Father, don't you see it's such an archaic belief to think I can't take care of myself and must rely on someone else to protect and provide for me? I'm fully capable of being in control of my own destiny."

"Have you had any food since coming on board?"

The question was quietly asked and yet pointed directly back to her and her fairly recently voiced claim to be able to take care of herself.

"Ummm..."

"Come, you'll stay in my rooms. We'll get you some food and talk about this need for independence."

"Yes, that's exactly what I am—independent."

"I thought you didn't want to be placed in a box?"

Dang, he had her there, but she wanted to be reliant on herself, not others, and that person is independent.

"Right. First, I'll ask you this only once. Are you sure all of this displeasure with your pathline is not because you don't look the same as all the other young women on Zandia?"

She had to think about her answer before giving it, they both needed to know the truth to this question. Looking down, she thought about how very different she was and how it may or may not have played a part in the risky chance she was taking.

"No, I'm comfortable with who I am, and don't mind how I look different from my peers. Appearances aren't everything."

He watched her closely before nodding, she thought, with an aura of pride surrounding him and motioned her forward.

"Fine, let's go."

Part I: Marked

Chapter One

Five Years Later

Sitting in her living space looking out the large picture glass window at the city view she now thought of as home, Sui Erom allowed her mind to slip back to the time she'd spent with her father after leaving her home planet. It had started as an act of desperation, sneaking onto his transporter, and had ended with her holding on to treasured memories. The time spent with her father had been the first and only period in her life she'd ever had with him alone. There was nothing more special for her, nor would she trade away one second.

When she'd snuck onboard his official carrier, Sui'd had no plan, didn't even know where her father was heading on his latest mission on behalf of Zandia. It hadn't mattered. She'd been sure any place was going to be better than home, where her pathline had dictated she go where she didn't want to. In the end, the experience had been more than she could ever have dreamed.

Even better, Lady Luck had been her companion. Her father, Ambassador Ero Seccus, had been sent to take a new posting on Earth for a four-year period. This was a usual occurrence, him leaving for long periods of time. Her mother always went with him, but this time there had been an emergency with her parents and she'd remained behind until it was all settled.

She'd always understood her father was important and therefore a busy man, but she'd be forever grateful he'd made time for her, listened to her, and helped Sui find her own pathline. They'd talked of many things, agreed on some and not on others. Her views on Zandian society—how messed up, behind-the-times beliefs opened them up to ridicule and lack of respect from others in the Universe—were ones she'd been surprised to find they had in common.

During their first meal together, they'd returned to her reasons for being on his transporter, leading them to touch on the state of their society.

"Nations constantly reevaluate themselves and where they stand within the time and the developments made. Despite what people think, there is no utopia for everyone. There is, however, a suitable medium. In fact, Sui, you can guarantee there is always going to be someone or some group left out. It doesn't make it right, but it does make for a more peaceful existence for society in general." The subject matter was something her father knew quite a bit about and she'd listened carefully to what he was saying.

"If we've "reevaluated" ourselves, then why are we still stuck with these outmoded beliefs?" It didn't bother her to show her confusion to him, not in the midst of their changing relationship.

"I don't have an answer for that, although I think when a planet decides to hold their traditions close, there's little room for advancements. In my opinion, there'll be a problem somewhere down the line. King Rore was never meant to take the throne and hadn't planned on it either. The years of his rule have been static, nothing suggested and therefore, nothing changed. Between us, I think he argues with his heir to find a mate in a bid to bring someone more youthful, enthusiastic and prepared to make changes to the throne."

After a long silence, Sui looked up at her father and, with tears in her eyes, told him what was in her heart.

"You realize you've never spoken to me like this before, as if I were a person who had a brain and cared about the state of our nation. You're treating me with respect and acknowledging my ability to have a stance on these important issues. This, amongst other things, is what I wanted at home but it wasn't an option."

She'd watched with tears flooding her eyes as he'd reached across the table and held her clenched fist.

"I understand."

The next day he started to teach her how to speak and write English. She'd loved seeing how astonished he'd been when he realized how quickly she picked up the language. He began teaching her other skills as well, such as etiquette and unique customs for various planets. Unbeknownst to her, he'd been grooming her, giving her tools to be able to work and support herself somewhere other than Zandia.

Sui smiled and sipped her hot cup of black mort, taking the time to slowly ease herself into heading off to work. The happy memories comforted her this morning. It hadn't been all work. She remembered how they'd spent many a day in front of his computer and watched speedball games from various sectors of the Universe, debating tactics and team selections.

It wasn't shocking that they shared enjoyment of the beloved sport. Speedball was a Universe-wide sport, and everyone was a fan. Each planet had leagues, playoffs, trials, whatever it took to compile the best national team possible. There were many knockout competitions played leading up to the big event. Every six years, the best teams converged on Earth for the pleasure of competing for a cup and, more importantly, bragging rights of being called The Universe's Best Speedballers.

She laughed out loud, thinking how she'd surprised her father during one game when she'd voiced lust for a couple of players. As quickly as the laughter came, she once again became thoughtful when she remembered how the conversation had progressed. It had started out being about sex and ended with his giving her something she hadn't known she needed, acceptance for being herself.

"Have you had a sexual encounter yet?"

"Father!"

"Well, you think this player is hot and another is kissable. I figure, even though you were on the emotive path, you might've been sexually active. I need to be sure you're prepared for what could happen. Men can be rather rough and uncommunicative when lust is riding them."

"No, I haven't but I'm sure I'll find a man I want and who wants me just as much."

"You're lucky Sui, not all young women are as comfortable in their skin as you are."

"It's the one I was born with, not much I can do to change it."

"Would you—change, I mean—if you could?"

"No, I wouldn't want to be anything other than me. I'm different and that's fine. There are times I wish I were taller, all the men back on Zandia prefer women who are tall and have thin muscular frames. When I stand beside a man I often feel like an overweight child, and I'm sure my appearance doesn't inspire sexual feelings."

"Don't be so quick to judge the male species. They're intelligent beings who, unfortunately, often listen first to their bodies, and only later to their hearts or brains. Remember, like women, not one is the same as the next."

Sighing deeply, she felt the inevitable sadness at being far away from home and her fold, her closest family members, settle over her like a chill. Her mother was a traditional Zandian woman, there to make her path-mate's life easier and therefore more fulfilling. In relationships like theirs, the man moved on to his companions for sexual satisfaction once the usual three children had been conceived. The Seccuses were different in that they'd remained together, despite not being able to have any more children beyond Sui. She liked that about them both.

It was clear to her now, she'd never have survived long on Zandia living true to the pathline chosen for her. Here on Earth, she felt secure and confident in her ability to live through her own hard work. It pleased her to be able to make this declaration. Who knows, maybe it was being older, but on this planet she interacted with men on equal footing and not from a position seen as beneath them.

She'd even taken a lover.

Sui giggled into her cup. No one from home would recognize her now, she appeared even less like a Zandian woman than she had before. She blended in with everyone else and liked that very much.

There was no doubt in her mind, the time spent with her father had been everything she'd needed. Last year, when the time came for her parents to return to Zandia, Sui'd remained behind on Earth. Unlike other occasions when she'd said goodbye to them, this farewell would most likely be the last time she'd ever see them. On the other hand, she'd also felt oddly happy to know her father meant something more to her than he had before this adventure. They'd made a connection on their journey here that she'd always remember fondly.

Standing up, she made her way into the kitchen, rinsed out her cup and walked back into the living space. Picking up her bag, she checked to make sure she had everything she needed and made her way out the door.

Life was good and about to get better. The Universe Speedball Cup competition was in town and she was working it.

Chapter Two

"Wearing number one..."

A deep and sultry voice resonated around the enclosed arena, beckoning men's cocks throughout the audience to harden with hope for a more personal touch. Smooth and deep, the Zandian translator brought pleasure through her voice to those who might not understand or want to listen to the verbal commentary in English. For this match Zandia's team was the home team and being introduced as they came out onto the hard floor of the arena.

"Wearing number two..."

The shock escalated exponentially once word spread through the supporters, mainly men, how it was a real woman, not a computer simulation, they were hearing.

Zandian women were a rare sight. They seldom, if ever, went off planet. And if they did, it was with a path-mate. Also, there was the point that a mated female would never be so disrespectful to her fold, clan or king as to do something as menial as work. To make matters even more outrageous, this particular woman was employed within a male-dominated field. It was outrageous.

Where was her fold leader? Even worse, what could her mate be thinking to allow such an outrage to take place? Were all questions being bandied about.

Instead of the focus being centered on the court and the teams, attention raced around the facility in search of the booth where the woman with the voice of pure seduction sat. The desire for a glimpse of a beautiful, bald and fit woman this far from home led a few men to go to such lengths as to stand up in hopes of being the one to locate her first.

Because of their size, the Zandians were always considered the team to beat. An average height for the men was over seven feet and the women came in shorter at six and a half feet. Universally they were tall, add their intense desire for physical fitness and strength, and you had a rotating team of five finally tuned athletes.

"Wearing number five…"

As returning champions, the Zandians were given a short schedule, two wins and they were guaranteed a spot in the semi-finals. A week into the competition and this was their first match. As usual, there was a large contingency of supporters who made the long journey following their national team to watch them play to win.

"Do you hear that voice?" Even in the locker room there was a sense of awe over the sultry translator's voice.

The wonder felt about the seductive power the voice held over the players was obvious. The not so secret desire for more from the woman tempting their desires shot through the men, who, moments ago, had been an aggressive bunch eager to start play.

"Shit! I don't know if my dick is hard from hearing our mother tongue being spoken perfectly or if it's the woman I'm picturing behind it." Surprised at his body's response, the player tried to ignore his building erection.

"Hard? I'm going to come standing here if she says one more word!" The athlete started to rub his hand over his dick, which was trying to push through the tight material of his skin suit.

"If these stupid uniforms didn't zip up the back, I'd get hold of my cock and give it a few good strokes to ease this hard-on. It's stupid to not have any sexual aides readily available back here." Fury and frustration had the man pacing up and down the tunnel, not sure he could wait for relief until after the match.

It wasn't so much anger as disgust lacing his words. It was the woman's fault, encouraging them all to feel something they weren't asking for, not when there was no relief in their immediate future. No, none of them liked having little control over their bodies' reactions in this way. The woman's voice took them captive as it trilled throughout the arena.

A physically sensual race as a whole, Zandian men didn't ever deny their pleasure, even for a moment. In fact, the main reason they were the butt of many jokes around the Universe stemmed directly from this area of their culture. No matter what they were doing or where they were, if their sexual desires rose, they'd summon a mate, companion or a sexual aide to take in the manner they wished, thinking only of their physical needs.

The most embarrassing, and unfortunately well-publicized, incident happened during a meeting between an ambassador and the representatives for the Nazons, an all female society. The diplomat later admitted to having felt exceedingly turned on by the gorgeous women and called for one of his companions to take care of his needs during the conference.

For nine hours, the naked woman had kneeled beneath the table between his splayed legs and sucked him to completion more than a half dozen times. If the man wasn't building to climax or orgasming, the companion continued to hold his rod in her mouth. The ambassador lost all respect from the group of women he was dealing with. It wasn't entirely because he was seen as a slave to his lust, but at the same time, it didn't enhance his stance either. No, their refusal to deal with him, and by default Zandia, was a result of how he'd squealed like a girl each time he came. It'd been most unfortunate, for with his full knowledge, the meeting had been taped.

"Focus, men, focus! Keep your brains off your dicks and on the game! Think of Ambassador Todi," their captain called out, trying to bring his men's focus back to the game they were about to play.

"Wearing number ten..."

"Ha! That fool. But you feel it too, Xer. The hard-on you're sporting is difficult to miss! Shit, anyone who cared to look could see every ridge on my cock in this skin suit." The man standing beside his captain looked down at his own body with disgust.

Xer Rieh was captain and, even though he disliked the label, was considered the heartthrob of the team and even more, the image used to promote speedball Universe-wide. It didn't help he was also next in line to rule Zandia. The entire package brought women from all over to throw themselves at his feet in hopes of being attached to him in some way, or at least have one night of pleasure to remember. The fact he had no mate at a ripe age of almost thirty years was shocking and made his every movement even more gossip worthy.

There'd been a path-mate chosen for him, but it was quickly discovered officials had been bribed to make this decision. In actuality, she'd been better suited for the life of a sexual aide and had been sent back for training in this new area. Since then he'd maintained a collection of companions whom he had no qualms about sharing. Everyone in his circle knew there wasn't one woman he used exclusively, and they were all available to any of his friends.

For many years, he'd fought with his father over his lack of a mate, a mother for his children, all in a bid for him to ascend the throne, but he was in no hurry. The prince strongly believed he had a mate somewhere out there, and when the time was right, they'd meet. In the meantime, life went on. He was going to be a full participant and work on how he saw the best route forward into the future for Zandia and its people.

"Wearing number twelve..."

"I have a plan to get through this wicked deprivation and it's knowing the moment that woman steps before me, I'm going to take her up against the nearest hard surface and fuck her!" As Xer spoke, his large hand went down and clasped his hard-on, giving it a firm tug before reaching down farther to readjust his balls into a more comfortable position between his legs. "In the meantime, all this unspent energy is going to be poured out onto those measly little Tulisians so we can fucking win this match as quickly as possible!"

"Wearing number thirteen..."

"Are you speaking of marking her?" Surprise laced Rol's words.

"Wearing number fourteen...Rol Tunociv."

Applause burst down the tunnel but neither of the two remaining men paid it any attention. This would be the first time Xer had ever chosen to mark a woman and could be viewed as no small occurrence. Only those in the ruling family had the option available to them and it meant no matter whom the sensual voice may answer to, she'd be Xer's to take—where, when or however he wanted.

"Yes, I will assert the right to mark," he told his friend with confidence.

A stunned silence followed his decision. This was a step he'd never taken before and he didn't want to explain himself further. Besides, time was pressing, and there wasn't a minute to spare to talk further about this development. With a slap to Xer's back, his best friend took off down the tunnel where he was met by another loud burst of yelling and clapping.

Xer no longer heard the noise. His thoughts were now completely focused on the beautiful sibilant tones as they slid smoothly down and around the arena, teasing him. He had a picture of her in his head. She'd always ready and eager for sex, never caring where they were or how they expressed themselves as long as they both came gloriously in the end. His fantasy woman was bald, tall, fit and firm of body, and completely denuded of any hair.

Smooth as silk, perfect to match her voice.

"Wearing number fifteen...captain of the Zandian Zoolopeans...His Royal Heir Apprentice, Prince Xer III..."

There was no change to the voice. It had spoken his name as easily and straightforwardly as all fourteen before him. There was no extra showing of respect, no deference, nothing.

Fine, it would come later, after he'd buried his cock to the hilt in her sweet pussy.

Heading down the tunnel in a confident and controlled pace, Xer thought over and over again about how he would take this woman and make the erotic voice tremble, scream, loose its steady control.

Once he stepped out from the tunnel opening onto the court's hard floor, the roar of the crowd was deafening. Paying the adoration no heed, he placed his hands on his hips, spread his legs wide and looked around for where the woman would be housed. Quickly he spotted the fogged glass booth up near the rooftop and dead center in the arena. Xer stood there, ignoring the rising volume of the crowd, and stared straight at the box as if he could see the woman for himself.

The body that held and nurtured the sultry voice would be his until he said enough.

Chapter Three

Goodness gracious! The man was an incredible specimen of male perfection.

Sui blew out the breath she'd unconsciously held when the prince had finally stepped out of the tunnel. Strength and skill were obviously present, but there was quite a bit more to number fifteen than his name, rank and stats. She looked down to her desk and took in the team members' photos, and was immediately drawn to his.

Thick black eyelashes surrounded deep, browner than brown eyes, flashing with intelligence, determination and confidence. Physically there wasn't an ounce of fat visible within the skin suit. Tall, broad shoulders, tapered hips, and from there her eyes danced across the best-looking bulge she'd ever seen—big all the way around and rock hard. His legs looked like tree trunks. She lifted her eyes to the monitor and saw an ass worthy of more than a second glance. In fact, she felt it was flawless.

But what held her attention at the moment, was the clean bald head, an aphrodisiac to her true inner soul. She knew, except for eyebrows, there wouldn't be a single hair on his body or any other member of the Zandian team. Big, physically fit, sans hair was the true beauty in the eyes of her home nation, nothing to hide one's true self behind.

This was a man built to rule a nation poised to emerge as a major power broker within the Universe, worthy of being the future king for her home planet. If only he'd get on with it.

Keeping her gaze on the screen, she mentally flipped through the copious amount of material given to her in preparation for the job as a live translating announcer for the Zandian Zoolopeans. Being a fan of speedball she thought she'd been prepared for how handsome they all were. It was another matter when they're standing right there in front of her.

From the inception of the competition, organizers decided to emphasize the cultures of various planets present. One way of doing this was to ensure the national languages, as well as English, were represented. And so, here she sat, translating and watching gorgeous men run around in skin suits. This was a wonderful path she'd found herself traveling.

Of course she was a big fan of the sport and all its nuances, and with her grasp on both English and Zandian, she was the perfect selection as translator. But there was also a secret desire buried inside her to vicariously absorb something from home while she could.

All because deep down, in her soul, she missed Zandia.

Every day she thanked her father for his help in seeing her settled here on Earth. She'd had her name changed so it didn't trace back to her fold, and had an apartment and job that gave her the independence she'd sought. With a new persona, she'd settled into a new life before he left.

Her normal working day would find her in an office environment, using the universal communication skills her father had taught her. The main thrust of her work was to interpret documents for people who didn't understand the difficult Zandian language themselves. It was challenging and interesting work.

There were times when she missed the reassurance and ease seventeen years of knowledge in one place offered a person. The trade off was being treated like a woman with a brain and soul rather than merely a body. Sad she'd given up so much, especially her homeland, to have this feeling of being worth something.

Watching the players warm up on the court below, she had a few minutes to catch her breath before the game began. Taking a sip of water, she thought this planet was a wonderful, open and adventurous place to live for a young, sheltered Zandian woman. Here, female roles were often the same offered to men, bar the military, which was still mainly a male bastion and made it a horribly touchy subject. People here didn't like preferences to be made based on sex.

What didn't fit into this air of equality was how the society of her new home was prudish. When it came to the human body, which nature provided, they saw it as wicked and not to be seen or revered, much less enjoyed through sex. One lesson she quickly learned was to show any physical affection in public was a big no-no.

On Earth, taking a lover was serious and usually led to a lifelong commitment and offspring, where on Zandia, if on the traditional pathline, fuck buddies were common to have until they were matched with an established male for mating or as a companion. Sexual aides went straight from graduation to a community requesting them. In regards to the genders, the difference of philosophies for the two planets was so far apart she'd not been prepared for what it meant to be single here on Earth.

Once her parents had left and she was fully in control of her own life, Sui'd wanted to spread her wings and enjoy sex, without any ties. Regrettably the man she'd chosen to be her first in what she'd believed was going to be a major event in her life, turned out to be easily forgettable.

As had the sex. Lately she relied on her fantasies for the wildly fulfilling sex life she always dreamed of having.

Despite the differing approaches to having sex, Sui still would change little about her life here on Earth. Throughout her time here, she'd learned more about herself than she'd expected. Now she understood more fully that, no matter how much she missed home, she still wasn't entirely suited for either the emotive or traditional pathlines offered to her on Zandia. Unfortunately, it meant she could never have been truly and fully happy there.

Shame really because, physically speaking, the men back home were a great deal more to her liking than those she found here.

Skin suits didn't flatter every player, but their captain was born to wear such a revealing piece of apparel. However, Zandian men with their large fit bodies were the epitome of perfection and were shown at their best in these uniforms. It definitely made her think of a particular desire to experience the sexual prowess of a man from her own planet at least once in her lifespan.

Shifting in her seat, trying to ignore the pulsing beat pounding in her pussy, she fussed with the controls to double check they were set correctly. No matter how she tried to stop it, her mind wandered right back to her rapidly rising passions.

Taller than most every other species, handsome, a fit body no matter what their age, and confidence ground into their bones were a few of their more attractive points. If you happened to see one naked, and it was common with their practice of stripping down and having sex wherever they wanted, it was difficult not to notice how well-endowed they were.

Like here on Earth, a few of the more conservative nations eventually requested, when Zandians visited their planets or claimed territories, this impulse for sex be reserved for non-public spaces. This wasn't a problem, as by nature they didn't care where they got off as long as their desires were served. If they had to move into a closet for the length of time it took to come, so be it.

She squirmed in her seat as the unsettled feeling continued to build in her core. Outside of her dreams, she wasn't used to feeling this horny. Prince Xer's intense stare at the box where she sat, as if he could see her, had encouraged this and brought a heavy dampness between her legs. Crossing her limbs, she squeezed them together and tried to relieve some of the tension.

Okay, be honest with yourself, Sui, you wouldn't mind spending a few hours playing with Prince Xer's impressive equipment.

Giving herself a mental kick, she reminded herself he was Zandian, and a member of the royal family to boot, and for her it meant hands off. Besides, she doesn't look like a Zandian woman and therefore wouldn't be considered attractive to any of them.

It was very important for her to not let anyone know where she was originally from. She was sure it would only bring all sorts of trouble to her and her fold. To her knowledge there'd never been a female from Zandia existing away from home, on her own.

Looking down on the court, she found five tightly muscled bodies covered in black from neck to ankles, black traction foot pads on their feet, stood ready to play one of the most dangerous sports around. Man, oh man, the sight of all those slick bald heads brought her eyes open wide and her mouth to gape.

The game would be fast-paced and nuances could be easily missed if her attention wandered to a fine ass here or an impressive package there. Working with the two other translators, she called the names for both teams' starting group of five as they lined up opposite each other. The players positioned themselves to start the game by leaping up to grab hold of the first metal orb as it dropped from the ceiling.

From that point onwards, there'd be no stopping play, unless there was a serious injury, for a full period, with four periods in a complete match.

Sui didn't think the semantics of the sport were difficult, which made it even easier to play throughout the Universe. The simple definition was the first team to fill all eight holes, or the team with the most holes filled by the end of the full hour, won. But nothing in that definition gave a hint as to how extremely dangerous the game could become.

Looking down as they jostled for position, she thought it was obvious why it wasn't an effortless sport. The court was a big part of the challenge. The field of play consisted of one big hardwood bowl and at each end eight four-inch holes were placed randomly, mirrored on the opposite side. To score, the team who held the five inch metal orb ran down the court, dodging the other team who tried to dislodge the ball for themselves, all in a bid to thrust it into a hole, and have it stay. They ran along the floor, sloping walls, wherever they must, in order to gain the perfect angle to get up the end wall and push the orb into an empty hole.

The worst part was when the big strong men, wearing no protective gear, did the inevitable and fell back down to the hard arena floor. Shaking her head, she focused on the monitor as the first orb dropped from the ceiling.

"First orb is caught in the air by jumping Zoolopean, Tunociv. He tosses it behind him to Rieh, who takes it and runs straight down the center into their end of the court. Looks like the Zoolopeans are taking no prisoners today. Two Todlepos…no, one, is almost upon him. He leaps, and misses as Rieh steps up onto the side wall and one, two, three long strides along the end…SCORE!"

Sui worked hard to focus on the action below on the court as well as listen to the English commentator call the game in her sound plug. There was a rhythm they'd setup in meetings before the competition opened and she needed to hit her cues or miss the call. It was going to be extremely difficult to do.

This wasn't the best time for her to suffer with passionate urges. Besides the pressure of working a live translation and the results being beamed around the Universe was intense, there was no lover in her life to help release some of the sexual frustration. Using her hand on herself was never quite as satisfying as she needed.

"Fourth orb is dropped and both front lines jump up and… Oh, that has to hurt. The Todlepos co-captain is down, caught an elbow in the face. Todlepos Kisk comes up from the pile with the orb, he's running down to their end of the court, almost there and he's tripped, the orb falls free! Zoolopean's Rieh picks it up, tosses it to Stebbis, he runs down, straight arming a Tulisian as he goes. He hits the side wall and falls back down, leaving the Todlepos on the floor. Stebbis tosses it back to Tunociv who is undefended! He runs up the end wall and…SCORE!"

With a deep breath, she forced the imagined erotic snaps of her and the prince having wild sex together to the back of her mind and put all her focus back on the match below.

"It is the third period and the Zandian Zoolopeans lead the Tulisian Todlepos six to two. The match will resume in five minutes."

Taking a moment to ease her back and neck, she stood and stretched her arms above her head before bending over to touch her toes, while listening to the other two translators chatter back and forth on the common link about the match. An unexpected smile moved across her lips as it dawned to her. Somewhere her parents were listening to her call this match, and she knew they'd be proud of her achievements.

Many women around the Universe watched speedball competitions to see the athletes in their revealing uniforms. Sui enjoyed the sight of almost naked men as well. But, even more important, she was hooked on the sport and the skill it took to make even one, much less eight holes. The players wore no protective gear and with the hustling, fighting and tussling taking place, there were often serious injuries. When grown men defied gravity, as these athletes frequently did in order to scale nearly fifteen-foot high walls to press a small orb into a slightly larger hole, the landing was rarely without consequences.

Dangling with her head down by her knees, she wondered how she'd made it this far through the match with erotic desires continuously flashing across her mind. It was a new experience for her to be completely focused on something other than work. To have only one thing occupying her thoughts, and to have it be sex, just wasn't her.

As she stretched back up, Sui thought about heading over to watch the Pelokis play later today and possibly finding a strong man to take on her passions for the night. They were tall and could handle her height without problems. Back on Zandia she'd been considered freakishly small. Out in the rest of the Universe she was tall, at just under six feet.

Suddenly interrupting her musings was the voice of her supervisor there at the arena coming over her private communication line. She straightened up and stood there as if he was in front of her and listened carefully.

"Ms. Erom, the Zandian team requests you attend their evening event to be held at the Universal Sportswriters Hall directly following the match." Always he spoke to her politely, professionally, but at the same time, it was obvious he wasn't a friendly sort of person, at least not with her. He wasn't an Earther, so maybe he wasn't used to a woman being in this mostly male domain.

Quickly she moved a finger to press on the mic button of her sound plug in order to speak with her supervisor. "Sir, could you please pass on my apologies as I will not be able to attend."

"No, not acceptable. Declining a personal invitation to a party hosted by His Royal Heir Apprentice and the Zandian Embassy would be an insult, and embarrass Earth as host of the Universe Speedball Cup. You were told to clear your schedule, to be available during the entire duration the Zandian contingency was on planet. Private transportation is being made available to take you directly from the arena to the USH." He hissed down the line with what sounded like more than impatience in his voice.

"Oh, but sir, I'm not dressed appropr—" she tried again.

"I've been told the transportation arranged will take you home first and wait while you change, before heading over to the function. There will be an escort waiting outside your booth upon completion of the match, which is now one minute away from resuming."

There was no room to maneuver out of the party.

"Yes, thank you, sir," Sui grudgingly acquiesced.

Oh crumb, what was she going to do now? There was no way she could get out of this. Her saving grace was no one should be able to guess she was of Zandian descent. If they did, she'd be in serious trouble.

Chapter Four

The match ended rather quickly once the fourth period started. The Zoolopeans had scored twice in a few short minutes. Sui's breath was blocked in her throat and would go no farther as she looked at her monitor. The entire time she worked on completing her system shutdown and paperwork, Xer aggressively stood in the center of the court, with hands on hips and a fierce look on his face. He didn't look at anyone as they tried to interview him. Instead he stared up at her booth.

There was no way she could let any of these men, their captain in particular, know she was Zandian. Sui was positive nothing good would come from it. Life on Earth suited her and she didn't think she could go back to being a useless object back home.

Finally she finished closing everything down and readied herself to go down to arena administration and sign out for the night. She walked out of her assigned sound booth and abruptly pulled up short. Facing the door was the first man from her home planet, other than her father, she'd ever been alone with. Relatively alone considering there were still over two hundred thousand people within the complex, but the hallway on the upper floor outside her booth was empty.

Inferiority tried to take advantage of her moment of anxiety, but it didn't work. Normally she towered over other races, but standing beside this man, she was the small one and felt her feminine self join the lust working through her body.

The bald behemoth had his arms crossed over his bare chest, legs placed in a wide stance, and absolutely no softness visible. All he wore were sandals and a loose pair of black silk drawstring pants, which left little to the imagination. Obviously she wasn't able to keep her eyes from checking out his package either. When her gaze finally rose to collide with his, she was met with a black, hard stare, and lips pressed firmly together. He showed no signs of knowing how to speak or smile.

Pull yourself together, you can and will fool these men. It's one evening and you look nothing like a woman from home.

Taking a steadying breath, Sui concentrated on pulling her confidence back around her, pasted a smile on her lips and looked him straight in the eyes.

"You must be my escort. I'm Sui Erom." She chose to speak in English to help her deception and reached out to shake his hand in an effort to simulate cultures who greeted others in this manner. It was another twist on reality because Zandians didn't greet people this way; instead they kissed. Her prize for the effort was a deepening of the man's frown. Another part of her ruse was in using two names, women back home are only ever introduced by their first names, only on official forms would her fold name be necessary.

As she was about to pull her hand back, he finally stepped forward and gave it a brief, one-pump shake. The effort it cost him to not pull her close and kiss her in his traditional manner was obvious in the stiff way he held himself. There was a long way until the end of the night, but right now her subterfuge wasn't looking so difficult to pull off.

"By order of His Royal Heir Apprentice, I'm your escort, Rol Tunociv." His voice, deep and formal, rumbled over her already stretched nerves, as he responded back in English.

"Yes, yes, nice to meet you. Mr. Tunociv. Now I recognize you, number fourteen. Yes, you played an excellent match—three holes, I believe. Congratulations." Oh dear, she'd known who he was but had been so nervous, it hadn't registered. Best friend of the prince and second-in-command of the Zandian military forces. They were taking this escort thing seriously. It was all right, she was as well. "I need to go turn in my paperwork and sign out of the arena. Where shall I meet you?"

"I'll escort you through whatever processes you need to do before taking you home to change for the celebration. Zandian attire is requested, but if you have nothing suitable some will be supplied to you at the USH before the event."

There was no flexibility in this man.

Sui definitely hadn't been expecting this! On a daily basis, the women back home wore next to nothing—every woman without exception. Some ensembles were more daring than others, but in general, it was all see-through and skintight. Another hurdle, but she would overcome this one as well.

There was no point in arguing with this man. She had the impression it would be futile, better to save her energy for the bigger fight she felt sure was heading her way. Nodding, she led the way through the various hallways, tubes and panels. Her friendly attitude had her speaking and joking with those people she saw and knew as they made their way through the arena.

This freedom was a joy for her. There was no need to ask permission from the man controlling her life to converse on any level with another person or wonder if someone would walk up, place her up against a wall and take her as they were permitted to with a sex aide or available companion. The right to speak to others with approval would've been hers if she'd been chosen for the traditional path, but the rules attached to the emotive pathline wouldn't have allowed her to go out on her own.

Once everything required of her had been finished, she turned to the man who'd followed stoically behind her for the past thirty minutes.

"That's all I need to do." Sui smiled and spoke to him in an open and friendly manner.

"While you were speaking with your supervisor about your schedule, I made a transmission to arrange for a seamstress to be waiting for you at USH. She'll fit you with appropriate garments for this event. If you'll follow me?"

Rol didn't feel it necessary to inform her he'd included in the transmission to Xer the news of how the woman with the voice appeared to not be Zandian. He wouldn't have thought himself attracted to a woman with hair and big tits, but his hard-on from originally hearing her voice had only grown stiffer when she opened the door to her booth.

White blonde curls bounced around a sweet face, she had big blue eyes and nice full red lips. The entire package tempted him to reach out and touch, but he wouldn't, at least not yet. She wasn't as tall as he'd been expecting either, but what she wore made her appear to be mainly composed of legs and breasts. A short-sleeved top ending around her hips flowed down to a pair of leggings, which were not necessarily tight but form-fitting enough to show him she had curves. The shoes she wore had heels, although without looking too closely, he couldn't guess how much height they added.

As he followed behind her, Rol quickly realized what a cute tight ass she possessed as well. There was a nice little swish as she danced away with an uninhibited movement. Those long legs would be perfect wrapped around a man's waist or up over his shoulders.

Despite not being what they'd all expected, Sui Erom was no disappointment.

Far from it.

Surreptitiously sliding his hand down, Rol gave his dick a hard squeeze and readjustment as he smiled. His friend was in for a shock, and an excellent one too.

Using transportation made available exclusively for the on-planet Zandian embassy staff, the trip to the USH was quick and uneventful. The hall was located behind a grand historical façade and offered an assortment of rooms for a variety of events. This evening's dinner was to be held in the formal dining hall but he escorted Sui directly up the stairs to a private room where a seamstress from Suria met them.

Surians were noted for their fine fabrics and sewing skills. They supplied apparel for most the Universe and exclusively to Zandia.

"Strip, missy." Motioning wildly, the tiny woman spoke brusquely as she collected the tools she'd need to build her creation.

"I'm sorry, no offense, sir, but I will not stand naked before some strange man." After listening to her and taking in her stance, he believed she hid behind the concept of prudery for some unknown reason. He'd seen her checking out his cock so she couldn't be uninterested in the opposite sex.

Both sets of female eyes rested on Rol who gave up quickly. Time was ticking on and he knew it was only a whim keeping Xer from bursting into this room. With an overly dramatic sigh, he turned, moved toward the door and stopped.

"This is as far as I go." He held firm in his position.

"Oh for goodness sakes, I'm a translator not some murderer who needs to be watched at all times. Is there a fear I'll skip out on dinner? It would be rude and I'd never offend another person, much less a member of royalty, by doing something like that," Sui fiercely proclaimed.

"By order of His Royal Heir Apprentice, you're not to leave my sight." The words said it all, or so he thought.

Hearing the rustle of material behind him, he was tempted to turn around and take a peek at the blonde in all her natural glory.

"Well, technically I'm not in your view. Will you get in trouble, it being an order and all?"

He smirked. The woman may have used a sweet tone, but the words were snarky, spirited...adorable.

"No, Sui, I'll not be in any trouble as long as you appear in the dining hall on my arm and soon." Staring at the door wasn't difficult, listening to the clinking of fine chain mail behind him was fairly torturous considering his cock had been hard for far too long. The minute he deposited the fair lady into Xer's hands, he was going to bury his tortured tool into the closest companion he could find.

"There's no way I can wear this—I'm basically naked! How about if I wear my undergarments beneath?"

"Missy most certainly will not ruin my creation by putting those ugly things beneath it." The seamstress was obviously offended by the suggestion.

"You must figure something out. I don't mean to be difficult, but I won't step out of this room with my privates on show."

Her words were clear and stubbornly stated, and merely tempted him further to turn around and see her for himself.

Sassy too. Working hard to hold back his laughter, Rol heard much muttering, digging through bags, and finally the seamstress seemed to have found a solution.

"What about this fabric?" The encouraging and optimistic tone was now present.

"Ohhh, it's simply stunning. Do you think you can make something suitable for me to wear out of it?" Sui sounded so hopeful.

"Pft! I can make anything, missy! Officially, it won't be a Zandian national garb, although I think it'll be acceptable. I make it and then we see if sir at the door says okay. But if it doesn't pass him, the chain mail goes back on and without despicable underthings. Fair?" The craftswoman was compromising but stating quite clearly it would be one way or the other, neatly trapping the blonde.

Heavy silence permeated the room for some time and when he was going to call a halt to the ridiculous issue, he heard a soft acceptance offered.

"Yes, all right."

Why he didn't put on the brakes he'll never know, nor care. He was enjoying himself too much to think about it.

Twenty odd minutes later and he was no longer laughing. The two ladies had been twittering on about fashion, slowly driving him insane. The only aspect making this escapade bearable was her voice. No matter what she said, his cock jumped with pleasure.

Damn he needed to come soon.

"Time is ticking, ladies." He knew his friend would be anxious, and was very surprised he hadn't stormed into the room as yet.

"Yes, yes, we're almost there, sir." A few nonsensical sounds and finally, "Okay, sir, very patient sir, thank you. Now, turn around and let us know if this will be suitable."

Shit!

There was no way Rol could have been prepared for the vision she offered. Sui presented a simple statement of beauty standing straight and proud before him. A light, floating white silk garment swirled around her full lush form. There were hints of what her body possessed beneath the fabric but nothing obvious, except for her nipples. Those tips were incredibly tight, hard and poked straight through the lightweight fabric, shadows, hinting at their presence and deep hue.

This was one hell of a surprise, a first-rate one too. Xer was going to be taken aback. Rol couldn't wait another moment to see it all happen.

Coming forward, he grasped her hand and started leading her back to the door and out of the room.

"Hey, take it down a step, big guy!" Jerking her hand out of his, she turned back to the seamstress, leaned over and dropped a kiss on the older woman's cheek.

"This is a beautiful piece of work and I'm covered. Thank you very much." Her appreciation was thoughtfully and honestly offered.

"Missy looks very elegant." The older woman preened under the focused admiration.

"What do you call this design? It's special so it needs a name."

Rol could hear Sui was being truthful in her compliment, but also curiously stalling for time. Briefly he wondered why she found it necessary to do so. Most women leaped at the opportunity to dine with a prince, others would fall to the floor naked to be touched by a professional speedball player, but this little lady stalled.

He looked closely at the blonde and his body roared with need, and his patience neared its end.

Hands on hips, Rol watched the two women, trying desperately to hold back his growl.

"Six Turns to Love for missy, now she not shame her host with the disgraceful private coverings." There was a wicked gleam in her eyes as she gave Sui the name.

Snickering at the Surian's words, Rol came back and took hold of Sui's hand, and once again led her out the door, but not before sending the older woman a conspiratorial wink. She'd far surpassed the request made of her, and Rol would ensure she was compensated well for her efforts.

"Come on, Sui, it's past time you made an appearance downstairs. The festivities are awaiting your arrival." Now the time was at hand, he wanted to savor the moment.

"What?" Stunned, she unexpectedly tried to pull him to stop, but he continued on.

"Keep walking. You're the guest of honor for our first victory match celebration." He'd made that up. It didn't matter why she thought she was here, just that she was.

"What about my clothes, shoes...shoot, my bag?" She turned, ready to go back to the room to collect her things, but Rol kept walking. Using his hold on her hand to whip her back around and moving forward.

"Relax. They'll be collected and waiting for you once the evening is finished."

"A lady is never without her bag. This is wrong."

"Fine, fine! I'll arrange for them to come down to you as soon as we get settled into the hall. Now come on, we must hurry." This close to seeing his powerful friend brought to his knees, Rol wouldn't stand for any more delays.

"Are we late?"

"Yes! Six turns late!" His patience was now gone; her constant delaying was wearing him down. Zandians were never late, to the other party involved it could be construed as an insult.

"Sheesh, no need to get all pissy with me. There was just no possibility of me coming out before another person, much less a group of men I don't know, wearing nothing to cover my privates."

"I know. I heard all about your difficulty. Remember, I was the man staring at a door for nearly thirty minutes." There was a hint of humor tracing through his words. He struggled not to show how funny he thought her gripping her strait-laced manners closer out of nervousness truly was. He'd seen all sorts of things in his position with Xer, but she was by far the most entertaining.

"Oh yes, right. Sorry," she said quietly, although there seemed to be a lack of sincerity to her words.

"None necessary. Now, are you ready?" Stopping before a guarded closed door, he faced her and didn't think he could hold back his laughter one more moment, the look on her face was priceless.

"What for now?"

"To meet His Royal Heir Apprentice, of course." Rol told her this in all seriousness, it wouldn't do her any good to offend the prince.

"Shoes! I have no shoes on my feet. And my hair, I didn't get a chance to look at it in a mirror—it must be a mess."

"Nope, it's fine. Let's go in." And he meant it, she looked stunning. There was no way his friend wouldn't be turned-on even more by her appearance than he'd been by her voice. With this tiny woman all the usual preferences a Zandian looked for were thrown out the window. She wasn't bald, thin or athletic, but was sexy as sin.

Still holding her hand, Rol faced forward and waited for the panel to be opened by the guard standing there. They walked into a small reception room off the dining hall with only one man standing inside. Off to the left was Xer who, Rol noticed, was stunned at the vision Sui presented. His mouth slipped down to hang slackly.

"Oh fuck!" exclaimed the prince.

Chapter Five

At no point in all her wild imaginings had Sui ever expected to be in the presence of a member of Zandian royalty. In the back of her mind was the necessity to not embarrass her fold. It must be ingrained in her to act properly and not shame her family when presented such a situation. With Rol, she'd worked hard to appear as an Earther and thought it had worked, but suddenly wasn't sure she could go any further with the subterfuge.

Riddled with doubts about the deception she was playing, no matter how much it meant to her to remain on this planet, she knew trouble was definitely headed her way. To make things even more uncomfortable was the prince's nearly nude appearance in slinky loose trousers barely hanging on to his hips and sexy bare feet to match.

"What did I do wrong?" Taking a step closer to the large man standing like a rock at her side, she whispered her worry for his ears only.

"Nothing. You're not what he expected, that's all," he offered quietly as he slowly led her over to where Xer stood.

"Well nuts, I thought I looked all right in this beautiful dress."

Two steps and she stood before the future king of Zandia, who also happened to feature regularly in her dreams as the sexy man who gave her multiple orgasms.

Embarrassing, yes, absolutely. Pulling a fast one over the same man, one possessing incredible power, made the moment horrendous and terrifying. There were no second chances here, but thanks to her father, she knew most of the rules by which to play. And maybe well enough to get by.

With grace, she dropped into a woman's customary greeting for a royal Zandian. Feet close together Sui sank to her knees, and laid her chest and forehead on the floor before his feet with arms stretched out to the sides. She heard Rol introduce her using English and found it interesting he didn't offer the prince a hint as to where he thought was her place of origin.

"Prince Xer, Royal Heir Apprentice, may I present Sui Erom, the voice of Zandian speedball here at the Universe Speedball Cup competition."

The wait for the prince to acknowledge her seemed endless and when she heard a greeting in Zandian, she wanted to cry. It had been too long since someone had spoken to her in her mother tongue.

"Good wishes from Zandia to you. Please rise." The common greeting was spoken with feeling, although what emotion wasn't entirely clear.

Without paying as much attention as she should have, Sui planted a hand to brace herself as she moved to stand. It would have worked but the loose end of her dress had fallen over her shoulder and it happened to land right where she'd put her hand. How embarrassing, she sabotaged herself and couldn't stand without ripping the garment off her body. Two big hands clasped her upper arms and easily lifted her until she stood steadily on her feet.

Looking up into deep brown eyes, she sighed and knew there was about to be a serious fight with her lustful libido.

Ha, get over yourself, this is a man way, way out of your league, and don't forget you're not a typical Zandian beauty either.

The little pep talk gave a boost to her confidence and she accepted getting through the evening's event may not be as difficult as expected.

"You're Zandian," the prince said with complete and utter confidence in his claim.

"Sir, I'm an Earther, but thank you for the compliment to my communication skills." The smile remained but it took effort. Right off the bat, he rattled the cage holding her nerves in check.

"Do you have a mate?"

"No, sir, I'm unattached." Oh dear, this was getting complicated.

"Where is your fold leader?"

"My father, sir? Ummm, he's no longer here." She sucked at lying. However, technically he was no longer here—on Earth.

There was silence and she had a moment of doubt about whether or not he believed her.

"You are very beautiful. You have a wonderful set of locks on your head and other attributes saying you're not from Zandia, and yet I know you are."

It was clear he wouldn't be easily swayed from his stance, but if she could make it through this one evening it would all be fine.

Normally self-assurance such as what the prince displayed would bother her, but in this case she found it a turn-on. To make matters worse, he was gorgeous. She wasn't sure what to say to his statement. It was flattering and yet if she wasn't careful, any misstep would drop her right in it.

"Thank you again, sir, for the flattering remarks, especially considering I don't remotely resemble what I understand a beautiful woman from Zandia would look like." Hopefully stating the obvious would bring his attention back to where she wanted it, the superficial veil she wore to cover her true self.

"Enough of this nonsense. Don't call me "sir", my name is Xer. Now, shall we go in for dinner?" The annoyance in his voice made it clear he wasn't convinced but would let it slide for the moment.

"Certainly, sir...oh, I mean Xer." She kept the easy smile on her face, although inside she was a molten mass of nerves.

"Rol?"

The other man stepped over and opened the panel she assumed would lead into the dining hall. Prince Xer reached for her hand and put it on his arm, held it there with his other one and led her forward.

An orgy was the best word for what they walked into. A wild cornucopia of lust was taking place before her very eyes. Zandia offered these types of scenes everywhere. Back home there was no sense of privacy when it came to sex. Although, in all fairness, this was the first time she'd seen so many people involved at one time. Usually it was a couple here or there groping on the street or on a public transporter.

The sounds echoing around the room were rather raucous. Moans followed vocal shouts of encouragement, grunts led easily into the slaps of hot sweaty bodies madly fucking. There wasn't much that surprised Sui, especially when it came to the physical phenomenon called sex. In fact she found the act rather beautiful, even, she supposed, when done like this.

While Prince Xer led her toward the head of the table, she found it difficult not to take note of all the activity happening along the way. It appeared the majority of the team members present were seated at the long table with only two not having made it to their seats before they indulged their sexual needs. One had his woman up against the wall and was thrusting seriously in and out of her, while the other made it to the table but had laid his companion on top and had her legs spread wide while they fucked.

Most of the other men had women kneeling on the floor between their legs, noisily sucking them to completion. The prince informally introduced each man by name as they walked down the room, and they nodded politely in return.

What was new to Sui was the centerpiece on the long table and her eyes involuntarily kept flicking back to see more. Two women appeared to be the entertainment for the diners as they mutually pleasured each other. The men avidly watched the duo, occasionally stroking a hand over the bald head working between their thighs.

As they made their way to the end of the table, she tried very hard not to look at any one place for too long, she was sure showing either interest or shock would lead to trouble.

Think of yourself as an ambassador for Earth. Don't judge, or condone, walk the middle line as cleanly as possible.

Unfortunately her little pep talk was too little, too late.

From the moment he heard her voice, Xer had been sure she was Zandian. And, despite the more obvious differences once he saw her in person, he was still sure of it. The sexy little morsel at his side hadn't flinched at the sight of his men's debauchery, and furthermore, she hadn't blushed either. No Earther would be able to carry indifference off so effortlessly.

No, he was right, there was no doubt about it.

He should be angry she was on her own, instead curiosity held sway. Why was she here, on her own and working, appearing and claiming to the world she was an Earther? How had she managed to leave without her father or fold leader reporting her missing?

Who was she?

The biggest surprise to him was how he found her mop of silky white curls captivating. It was difficult to restrain himself and not bury his fingers into its depths and test their softness. There was no hurry; it would happen soon enough. All he had to do was hold on to his patience. Sounded easy, but wasn't sure it would be.

Dismissing the waiting attendant with a wave of his hand, Xer pulled out the chair next to his and waited for her to sit before settling the seat beneath the table and taking his own. Rol nodded to him and took the seat on the other side of Sui.

Xer knew the man was in a bad way, but he was his best friend and most trusted right hand, there was no other person he could've sent to ensure this woman's presence at his side tonight. Already Rol's leggings were untied and his cock bursting free. Before he had fully sat down, a traveling companion was positioned between his legs and had her mouth open, ready to receive his friend's ready-to-explode erection.

It was going to be trying on his control as well, but Xer was determined to wait as long as it took for this woman sitting at his side to settle down before making his move. He wouldn't want to frighten her, although there was no doubt he would mark her this evening.

Taking a closer look at the petite woman, he noted her surreptitious interest in the centerpiece as he waved away the woman waiting to relieve the pressure of his obvious hard-on.

No, at the moment he was far too entranced with the gem beside him. Her generous, bouncing breasts were very enticing. He was sure they'd be sensitive and very responsive. The tips were visibly hard and being slightly jostled in the soft fabric of her gown.

Although he would've preferred to see her dressed in the traditional fine chain mail he requested, her attire was no less erotic. Bare, silky-looking, white skin was visible in flashes, hinting at what she would look like completely nude. The fabric wrapped around her hips, further enhancing her curvy shape and peach-like ass. Earlier, when she'd gone to her knees to formally greet him, Xer'd been hard-pressed not to drop down behind her and take her then and there.

Looking around the hall, he noted the last two men had finally taken their places at the table, allowing their chosen companions beneath the table before taking their seats. After giving the attendants a few moments to ensure everybody's glasses were full, he stood to make a toast.

"Congratulations, men!" His voice boomed down the table. "We played well this first match, and we never doubted the outcome. Now, with honor I introduce to you the owner of the sibilant voice that, before the start of the match, had us all so hard we didn't think we could move out onto the court to play. But you're all great speedballers and were able to funnel all the excessive energy into a victory."

Reaching down for his glass, he raised it in salute to the beautiful woman at his side. All his men stood, some shooed away their suckling companion, leaving their large rods standing tall, shining from the attention they'd been receiving, and others allowed the women to remain rooted to their dicks.

"To the scrumptious Sui." His voice was deep and rumbled as he turned lust-filled eyes to hers.

"Yeah! To Sui!"

A cheer went up. After the men finished their beverages in one swallow, they waited for Xer to sit before they each sank back down into their chairs. Attendants moved quickly to replenish the men's glasses with a sparkling energy drink full of nutrients and vitamins.

"Thank you, gentlemen, and I look forward to calling your remaining matches, all the way through to the championship." She spoke clearly and loudly enough to be heard over the various sucking noises.

"Yeah!"

He noticed she hadn't stood up but did raise her glass to those around the table. His eyes trailed around and wondered if she was shocked by how easily the men met her gaze as their pricks continued to receive personal attention from another. One man was a little out of sync and shouted with his completion instead.

Out of the corner of his eye, he watched her take a small sip before she looked to her right to speak with Rol and found him occupied stroking his impressive length into a companion's mouth. She turned to her left and was caught by his gaze.

Xer didn't like how he was her second choice, and yet on the other hand, was pleased to note how there was a faint blush to her face. He accepted she was getting turned on by his men's salacious actions and decided not to press his assertion of her origins and instead continue on the road to marking her as his.

Dinner was supposed to be a formal and dignified affair, and yet the mood was relaxed and heated, helped by the fact the centerpiece remained intertwined for the men's enjoyment. As was usual in these after game events, there also seemed to always be some man fucking a woman to a screaming pitch. Xer noted Sui seemed to be absorbed by the activities of the two women. She didn't come across as a companion or sexual aide, and he quickly figured the activity was most likely not something she'd seen back home. It didn't take long for him to come to understand she wasn't very experienced in the traditional paths, and yet she seemed to be showing interest in sexual scenarios around her.

Sui Erom was a paradox. She appeared very naive, unaware of her sexual appeal, to such an extent he wondered if she was still unbroken. And yet neither did she shy away from the open play as an emotive pathline woman would.

It was going to be a pleasure to discover all her hidden depths.

Chapter Six

"Do you have a man in your life, Sui? What are they called here, a boyfriend?" He looked at her as he asked the simple question.

There'd been nothing easy about this evening. Granted she was treated very well and would normally have enjoyed the loud and untamed actions and conversations of the men, but she was nervous about giving herself away, so was more restrained. She continuously looked for a trap in every question from this man.

"When there's time I date, but recently work has been keeping me busy." She felt secure in answering with the truth.

"What a shame. A woman as beautiful as you should never lack for personal attention, especially in the physical way."

Ahhh, seduction was his game. Sui wasn't sure if she had the strength or willpower to deny him. There was also the fact that she wasn't entirely sure she wanted to turn this man away from her bed.

Xer looked up with a thoughtful look on his face. She should've braced herself for the unknown and unexpected. There was no way she could've prepared herself for the next question.

"Do you have a fuck partner?"

There was an innocent look on his face as he asked the question, causing her beverage to unintentionally come spraying out of her mouth and all over him. Considering the edge of lust she'd been riding all day, she felt her luck had finally been used up.

"Oh dear, I'm so sorry, Xer." Using the loose edge of her dress, she reached over and dabbed the liquid from his face. This close up she found him too handsome for her own good. The pulse in her pussy had not stopped beating all day. The moment she touched him, she squeezed her legs closer together, making an effort to alleviate the growing need.

It was useless. Since before the match began she'd been suffering, and now, she lost all her common sense. There was no stopping this passion train now. Closing her eyes, she leaned up and laid a gentle kiss on his mouth. They were wonderful firm lips, parting almost instantly beneath her mouth. Unable to deny herself the hunger for more, Sui snaked her tongue out to trace the opening and pulled in her first taste. The flavor was cool, fresh and sweet from the fruit he'd been eating.

On a groan, she took the hand holding the edge of her dress to dry off his face, dropped the fabric and slid it over his smooth dome. Pulling his head closer allowed her to deepen the kiss.

She pushed her tongue into his moist cavern quickly, but took the time to trace the tip along the roof of his mouth, drawing a moan from him. He grasped her around the waist and lifted her onto his lap. She opened her eyes in surprise and saw determination on his face but felt no fear. Right then she knew nothing was going to derail her from having this man riding between her legs before the evening was finished.

At least once in her life, Sui wanted to experience the full physical possession of a Zandian man. Right now, this one wanted her. Granted he was much more than she'd expected, but he turned her on and lust was the emotion driving her now.

Sprawled across his lap, she gladly gave herself over to him. She closed her eyes and fell further into the experience of passion-filled play. She'd started something and didn't feel fully equipped to finish, so Sui gladly laid back and let him take control, eager to enjoy the sensual adventure.

Their lips locked together, tongues dueled, curled around each other. For the first time in her life, she was feeling free enough to enjoy all the pleasure her body was pleading to indulge itself in. Her arms moved to wrap around his neck, giving her purchase, and arched her body up, rubbing her eager breasts over his firm chest.

The fabric she'd earlier begged for was being slowly unwrapped from around her breasts. She felt each layer being removed and wallowed in the erotic undressing this man treated her to. When the final layer was gone and her chest was exposed to the air, she released his lips and moved back, opening her eyes to look into those of the man who held her with purpose.

What she saw left her feeling like a treasured and wanted woman. His lush brown gaze was glued to her breasts. She couldn't help the deep breath and subtle bowing of her back, which, by default, offered the mounds up for his attention.

The longer he looked upon her and didn't touch, the more unbearable the wait became.

"Please."

"What do you want?"

Oh no, he was going to make her say it. Could she? Did she know what to ask for? If it meant easing the desperate hunger rapidly rising between her legs, then yes, she'd do whatever it took to find relief.

"I ache. Help me please."

A large hand smoothed down her neck and over her breasts, where he cupped one. He squeezed the handful, causing a big tight nipple to spill out between two fingers.

"Where do you hurt, baby?"

His long tongue stretched out and licked the excited tip like it was a sugared treat. The damp muscle flicked the tightly pointed nipple, teasing her desires even more. She groaned, thrust her chest higher and wished her legs were free to spread wide and invite him to dabble between them, but they remained covered and wrapped in fabric.

He carefully held her head in one hand while the other continued to manipulate her breast, bringing her frustration level to ever higher peaks. Groaning, she watched as he ran the flat length of his tongue back and forth over her hard nipple.

"Please, more. I need more of your mouth...on my...breast."

"More I can definitely do with this delicious tit." He readjusted his grip on her breast until the pebbled point rose high above his fist. After a few torturous licks, he slid his mouth over the reddened tip and softly suckled while holding her gaze with his own.

Did she moan because of the look in his eyes or was it because he looked incredibly sexy latched on to her breast? It didn't matter when he increased the pressure and she felt her nipple harden further under his attentions.

In minutes, she'd become a purely sensual woman, one capable of pleasuring and being pleased in return, exactly as it happened in her dreams. But still she needed much more to pacify the desire building inside her.

61

Moving her hands from around his neck to his ears, Sui tugged at the same time she thrust her chest higher, trying to bury her breast deeper in his mouth.

"Harder, I beg you, suck harder!"

"Ummm."

The force from his mouth increased until it almost hurt, only it was so good. His pulling on her breast tugged on a line that was connected to her pussy, making her need more urgent. She groaned, intense bliss flooded her senses, and yet she still reached out for even more.

"Please, Xer, bite me."

Opening his mouth wide, he used the side of his back teeth and gently bit down, imprisoning the excited tip. In an instant, she lost all of what remained of her composure as he ran his teeth over the hard point.

"Just like that, oh yes!"

He was gorgeous, and even more stunning when having his way with her breast in his mouth. Would she be able to handle him fucking her?

Definitely!

With his ears still held hostage, she tried to encourage him to explore her further. Her hips moved but the motion brought her back down from her bowed position, stretching her nipple from the grip of his teeth.

"Uhhh...yes..."

His strong mouth opened and moved back over the large red nipple and sucked deeply, his tongue stroking, soothing the distressed tip. She felt no need to hold back her appreciation of what he was doing to her, not when he was humming with the pleasure of his task.

"Hmmm." With a loud wet pop, he released the nipple. "What a lovely set of tasty tits you have, my petite Sui," Xer offered on a rough rumble as he kissed his way over to her other breast and treated it to the same hard suckling.

She couldn't find it within herself to release his ears. His smooth dome called to be stroked but his ears spoke louder to her, they were perfect for her hands to hold on to while he feasted upon her breasts. It felt like she was holding him there, where she wanted him most. Only she knew he was there because he wanted to be, not because she had the strength to hold him there.

It wasn't long before she was begging. The desperate need rising in her pussy was unbearable. With her legs pressed close together, Sui could feel the moisture gathering, seeping down her upper thighs. She'd been reduced to a groaning mass of femininity squirming on the future king of Zandia's lap. Not to mention they were in a room full of people. But her mind skimmed right over all of those inconsequential things, and instead stayed focused on the pleasure she was receiving and easily sank into a pleading mode.

"Please, please, I'm begging you to…uhhh…"

There was no doubt he was enjoying himself. Beneath her hip, she had no problem feeling the large stiff rod she knew would soon be fucking her cleft. Would he fit or was he too big, and would therefore be an insufferable taking?

Suddenly she was shifted from her place on his lap before he stood them both up. Disoriented, she found herself pressed between the table and Xer. Standing on her tippy-toes, Sui reached up and wrapped her arms around his neck, bringing him down to meet her kiss. His erection bumped against her belly, leaving her even more eager to be filled by the impressive tool.

There was a slight tug at her waist but she thought nothing of it, enjoying the feeling of her tight nipples rubbing against his smooth, hard muscled stomach.

Strong hands clasped her hips, stroked along her flanks and moved around to cup her generous ass. He didn't shy away from their size, instead he squeezed as if testing each cheek's suppleness. Rough fingertips reached between her legs and teased her damp opening.

"Oh yes, Xer, yes..." Her head dropped back and hung without any support. Sui lifted a leg up to rest upon a solid hip and curled it around to rest beneath his taught ass, pulling him close. He tempted her further by bumping and grinding his thigh against her pussy.

This was the moment she realized they were both nude.

Hands that had been gentle in their teasing now held her firmly, as they effortlessly lifted her onto the edge of the table. In surprise she reached out and used her hands to brace herself and looked up only to be snared by the intense passion reflected in his eyes. There was no turning back. And at this point, she didn't want to either.

"My sweet petite Sui, spread your legs for me, show me your enticing pussy."

With one leg still resting on his hip, she moved the other up so it too sat on him, then shifted them both up higher to rest about his waist. While moving around, her tits teased him and held his attention while she adjusted herself, but once they settled, his gaze sank to her mound.

"Look at this lovely, silky blonde pelt. Fuck! The little patch looks like an arrow pointing straight down to the pinkest, most lush pussy I've ever set eyes upon."

She looked down and watched as he pushed a big finger deep inside her cleft. A long groan slipped out of her lips when

64

the digit curled and stroked along a patch of nerves she hadn't known existed. Instantly her head fell back and she clenched her muscles hard to keep him inside her.

Feeling like she was about to loose herself within the lust building inside her, she tried for one last bid of control and brought her head back up and looked at him. She was shocked to see him bring the finger dripping with her honey up to his mouth and suck it clean. What an erotic and intoxicating act, she hadn't been prepared for it and was lost.

"Mmmm, your cream tastes delicious."

"Take me, Xer. Please put this large dick inside me and fuck me." Teasing his senses in hopes of changing his current path of slow seduction, she moved her hand over his bare groin to hold his rigid hard-on and stroke its length as she spoke. It was an impressive cock but she had faith he'd wield the weapon in such a way as to grant her great unimagined pleasure.

As he climbed up onto the table to rest on his knees between her legs, she released her hold on his cock and dropped down to lay flat against the hard surface.

"I'm not going to take you, Sui." With a hand firmly holding his rod, he placed the crown into the opening of her slit and circled the opening while his thumb stroked her clit. "What I'm going to do is mark you as mine. Mine to take when, where or however I please, for as long as I want."

It took a few moments for what he said to sink in to her passion-laden mind. Gasping with shock, she opened her eyes wide.

What have I done?

Chapter Seven

Hands firmly holding her hips, Xer thrust his cock into Sui with one sure and steady stroke. He hooked her legs over the bend in his arms, dropped down to brace his hands beside her breasts and held his length buried inside her tight, pulsating slit.

The pleasure he found while buried down in her depths spun his mind out of control. Tight, moist heat surrounded his rod and it took an immeasurable amount of strength to not start plunging in and out of her until she screamed with pleasure. Wait, had he heard her scream? Suddenly he was sure she had. He looked down and was worried over the frown now gracing her beautiful face.

"Oh shit! Did I hurt you? Were you unbroken?" Fear raced through his mind. Had he harmed her in some way?

Her blonde head was shaking back and forth but he needed to hear her say she was okay before he could continue the ceremony. This was difficult, bringing the woman to orgasm three times before he himself could come would normally not be complicated. But he'd been hard since he heard her voice resonate throughout the arena. In the shower, he'd tried to relieve some of the pressure by using his own hand, but it hadn't worked. Not surprising when he knew the woman with the most incredible voice he'd ever heard was going to be his in a few short hours.

"Talk to me, little one, I need to hear you say you're okay." His worry was obvious and he didn't care. She was so small and he was out of his mind with need. Then the unexpected happened—the purpose of having her here beneath him shifted. Originally it had been a whim, but now it felt important, a need, he hadn't expected this shift. Despite this change, he couldn't stop.

Soft small hands moved up and wrapped themselves around his biceps as she began mumbling incoherently.

"What are you saying? Slow down, I can't understand you." Panic was running up his spine with the possibility she wouldn't want him to give her pleasure, to mark her.

"...take me...take me...please, fuck me...please..." She panted.

"All right, all right." Xer tried to soothe her but inside he was thrilled. Already he had her dancing along the rim of passion. There was no doubt she'd be wearing his mark by the end of tonight.

Five slow and shallow strokes were all it took to send her screaming over the edge.

"One!"

A loud cheer went up by the men standing around watching the momentous ritual take place. Neither participant entwined on the banquet table paid them any attention.

On Zandia, to watch a couple fuck in public happened all the time, but the marking ceremony was not a common occurrence and they were all excited to be there and watching. Besides, Xer might be their peer and teammate, but he was also heir to the throne. This was a significant moment to be a part of and none would ever forget being present.

Moving back to rest upon his heels, Xer spread his arms wider, taking her legs with them, and looked down to where they remained joined. Partially buried in her pussy, he was thrilled to see a hint of her lower lips stretched around his cock with her cream coating its visible ruddy surface. Her small blonde patch of hair felt delicious against his smooth groin and enticed him to pet the silken curls with his fingertips.

Rules for marking were old and each must be strictly adhered to. From the moment the rod enters the female's cleft the man isn't allowed any direct contact other than through his fucking to help bring the woman to climax. Nor could he remove his cock before all three orgasms had been achieved, to do so immediately ended the rite. At the same time, it didn't mean he couldn't entice her to help his cause by manipulating her body for him.

"Strum your clit for me, baby, rub this sweet nub begging for attention." He growled low, trying to keep control of his desire until he finished all the steps necessary to mark her as his. Successfully completing the ritual was necessary for his sanity.

One hand dropped from holding tightly on to his upper arm and smoothed down her belly, through her curls, until her first finger barely flicked across the tiny hard protrusion.

"Open wide, Xer..." She offered no other hint until she took the same finger and held it up for him, and he didn't deny her. His tongue curled around the digit, savoring the mere hint of her unique essence. He was nearly beside himself when she took the moistened digit and went back to work the bundle back and forth.

Now he fucked her. He made long, smooth strokes in and out of her slick pussy. In balls deep and back out until only the crown rested inside her heated slit. Without pause, his cock returned, fucking her with determination to bring her to a screaming orgasm once again.

"Do you hear how wet you are for me, Sui? Listen to how your soaking little cunt welcomes each thrust from my dick." Xer could see how his words affected his lover and was thrilled.

"Yes, yes, faster, move faster, please..." Her finger furiously stroked over her hard clit as he maintained a steady pace.

"No faster, a nice and even speed. I want to remember everything. Can you feel every inch of my rod as it slides inside you?" He would control this mad, lust-filled session—the outcome was too important not to.

"Oh yes, yes! So full when you're inside me, soo... Oh, oh, Xer, ungh!" Her sweet, hot box squeezed and released, squeezed and released along the entire length of his still hard rod. The clenching, pulling muscles followed by her scream of satisfaction, a siren's call and difficult for him to deny. He wanted to come. The desperate need to flood her with his seed was front and center in his mind, but he had to wait. It was not yet time to come, no matter how tempting.

"Two!"

"Perfect, fucking perfect. I love a screamer. Come on, baby, one more. Give me and my cock one more of those delicious, pussy-clenching orgasms of yours and you're mine." Victory was within his reach. Now he was in the position to demand one more climax and then she was his.

His balls felt big, hard and full of seed as they bounced off her ass with each thrust.

"Ungh, ungh!"

He fucked her hard and fast, pushing grunts of pleasure from her and thriving on each one. Back on his knees, he used his hips to keep her legs spread out, placed his hands flat on the table next to her head and started ramming his cock in and out of her amazingly slick slit. A trickle of sweat snaked down his back. Xer wanted this third climax badly. He needed to have Sui screaming with pleasure as he rode her, this vision gave him even more strength of purpose.

"Ungh, ungh!"

"Ummm, here we go. You like my fucking, don't you, baby? You love my cock!" Xer enjoyed a woman who was vocal while erotically engaged. It meant she was focused on them and the quest for fulfillment. To know she was there with him turned him on even more.

"Yes, take me, you big bald stud, yes, ungh..." Sui panted as he moved in and out of her clenching slit.

"Fuck, you're tight!" He growled.

"So deep, yes, ungh...Xer!" She was utterly lost to his lust.

She screamed at the top of her lungs as the third climax raced through her body, trying to pull him over the wall with her.

"Three!"

Sui wasn't done yet. Xer slightly relaxed his stance, ready to start shafting her because he was so close to coming. Instead she took him by surprise and tried to roll him onto his back. There was no way he'd do anything to hurt her, so he went with it and worked to ensure his dick stayed buried in her wonderfully warm and wet cleft.

She sat up straight, breasts thrust out and curls dancing wildly around her head.

"Oh yeah, baby. Right now, ride my cock right now!" This didn't usually happen. During the marking ceremony, he was supposed to be in control of the fucking, but it didn't matter, he'd achieved the required three climaxes. This was their rite and therefore perfect. If she wanted a taste of driving their passions, so be it.

"Like this? Is this what you want, gorgeous?" Holding her breasts, she rose on and off his rod far too slowly for him. He realized she was teasing him like he'd done to her, only he wasn't going to last long.

He reached out, clasped her hips and moved her exactly how he wanted it—hard, hard enough to allow her tits to bounce wildly. It didn't take long for her to move her hands to his shoulders and start taking all he freely offered.

As she came again, calling out his name, he quickly rolled her and started jackhammering his cock in and out of her spasming heated depths. In seconds, his dick started expanding, pulsing, shooting load after load of his cum deep down, beyond the mouth of her womb.

Leaning down, he kissed her as he came, giving her his seed and completing the ritual.

Satisfaction quietly threaded its way throughout his body and soul. He was sure he'd made the right decision in marking this woman.

"You, Sui, have been marked by me, His Royal Heir Apprentice, Prince Xer Rieh of the Roiroirepus Clan. You're mine to take how I want, when I want and where I want." He ground against her, causing his still hard cock to thrust even further within her slit, before he sat up on his knees. He pulled her hips up as well so they remained locked together.

Xer could see she was still adrift in her passion. No problem, he'd ground her to his side with the final step of this traditional Zandian ritual. Slowly he pulled his rod from her and grinned when she moaned over its loss. It also brought her eyes to his and he waited for them to slowly focus.

Once he slid his cock back into her heated depths, he moved one hand down and stroked her belly, making sure she was aware of how deeply he was buried inside her. Holding a hand out, he knew instinctively Rol was as ready for this moment as he was himself. When a mass of tiny black onyx beads strung together with an occasional bright aquamarine one and a slim, bullet-shaped piece of onyx at one end was placed in his hand, his smile grew.

The thumb on the hand stroking her belly moved down and worried her still trembling clit. Wrapping the thin wired hook on one end of the jeweled strand around her nub, he tightened it until she groaned, and squeezed it a little more, making sure it was secure. From end to end the strand was fringed with more beads dangling down in random lengths. The solid piece at the other end was held within his clenched fist as he continued to tease her trapped bundle of nerves.

Putting the cylinder shaped bead in his mouth, Xer looked down and held her attention as he sucked on the piece for a few short moments before he slowly placed the hard mass inside her slit. He felt how firmly she gripped the smooth jewel as he moved it without rhyme or reason.

He didn't look away from what he was doing, but nodded again to say he was ready for his friend's help. Rol effortlessly hopped up onto the table and settled on his knees behind her head. Reaching out, he grasped Sui's ankles and moved them until she was pulled off Xer's rod and nearly doubled over. Bodacious ass in the air and cheeks spread wide, revealing her tiny pink rosette, Xer thought the sight was temptation itself.

Pulling the onyx bullet from her grasping pussy, he chuckled. "Your pussy is eager to be filled again, little one, but don't worry. This onyx is for another place." Sliding the piece along her dripping seam up and around to her tight rose, Xer introduced the hard, pointed tip and steadily pressed against the opening.

"What?"

"Don't worry, I'd never hurt you. Trust me, Sui. Do you believe me?" Was he asking too much too soon from her? It didn't matter. He'd have her wearing his mark, now.

"Xer?" she queried.

"Relax, be easy, sweetheart. There, now relax, push out a little, ahhh, there, nice and easy..." He spoke to her using a soothing tone, trying to gentle her nerves.

Slowly, but insistently, he pressed on, offering calm encouragement when the need rose higher. Within a few moments, the slim plug was buried in her unbroken ass. He hadn't known how it would feel to mark a woman but was thrilled and pleased to find this woman unspoiled and ready for him to enjoy.

Leaning down, he dropped a soft kiss on each ass cheek before he gave his friend the sign to release his woman's legs. They fell naturally around his hips. He leaned over and took a nibble from each tit before he kissed her, possessing her mouth as thoroughly as he owned the rest of her body.

In one quick move, he stood on the table, tall and commanding while straddling Sui's nude body. He placed hands on his hips and looked around the room at every man present. He caught each of their gazes, determined they understand what he was about to say was significant.

"This woman wears my mark and is mine to have or to share, but mine first! Does everyone understand?" The stern look on his face matched the demand for compliance he expected.

"Yes, sir!" they answered in unison and full voice.

Lying on a hard table did have a way of focusing the mind, especially when one realized she was naked, had just been royally fucked—literally—before a group of people she didn't know, and marked as a possession.

Oh crap, how was she ever going to get out of this?

She looked up at the man straddling her. At the moment he appeared to be fierce and mean, a warrior, not the man who'd given her orgasm after orgasm. Her only other sexual experiences had left her wanting. Now she knew why—she was made for a Zandian man.

Turning her head, she noticed Rol was naked, dick hard and eager, kneeling behind her, smiling down at her.

Wait a minute, did he say to *share* if he wanted?

Oh man, she was in deeper trouble than she thought.

Part II:
Claimed

Chapter Eight

"Please listen to me. You are the Royal Heir Apprentice of Zandia and I am an Earther! Therefore, you can't mark me!"

Sui was extremely frustrated. She'd been sure he'd understand what she was trying to tell him, but he wasn't listening to anything she said, the big pigheaded man.

The look on his face said it all, whatever she said, he didn't believe. Xer Rieh of the Roiroirepus Clan had made up his mind of her origins before he ever saw her and what she said made no difference. They—she—had been circling the issue since she'd stormed out of the dining hall and back into the small reception room they'd met in.

It hadn't been a pretty picture either. She'd been completely nude, his semen dripping down her legs, and trying to get down from the banquet table with as much dignity as she could muster under the circumstances. There wasn't a muscle in her legs not quivering from their physical exertions. The prince had thoroughly fucked her and she admitted to enjoying every stroke. Later, when she was alone and could be honest with herself, she'd accept her mind and soul had flourished under his possession. Only this was not the time or the place for such a confession.

A moment of weakness was what she'd like to label the interlude with Xer, but in reality it'd been much more. Sui knew she missed home and her fold, desperately wanted a real and meaningful relationship with a man who pleased and pleasured her, but also respected and needed her in return.

Sui wanted more out of life than she was currently experiencing. Although, no matter how she looked at it, she still had more than if she'd remained on Zandia.

Maybe the leaders at NEI had been right, she should have followed the emotive pathline. A mate would be the perfect solution to satisfying her physical needs, however, it would break something inside her if it were a Zandian type relationship. The male figure controlling everything, no emotional attachment required. Deep down she understood it was the often desired emotion, love, she was looking for and wanted to have. Unfortunately this man was not only out of her reach, he'd also never be anything more than an owner.

From all the self-awareness ebooks she'd read during her time here on Earth, and there'd been many, she knew exactly who His Royal Heir Apprentice was, her heartbreaker. His handsome physique wasn't everything that drew her to be at his side, although the lust was definitely present. There was his intense sense of power and control, even now radiating off him in great waves, reaching out to pull her closer. She'd read news flashes from Zandia writing of his intelligence and forward thinking, two qualities she respected greatly. Sadly he was still a Zandian male who'd always look at her as nothing more than a body to enjoy.

Crossing her arms over her chest, she looked over at him with what felt like the weight of the world resting on her shoulders. She proudly stood before him, completely naked except for the beautiful piece of jewelry, his mark, which still kept her in a constant state of arousal. There was a fight going on inside her. One side wanted to rush to him and submit to the lust still looking to play, the other side wanted to escape with whatever self-respect she could muster.

"May I please have my clothes? I'd like to return home now." What Sui was sure of was getting out of this place and more importantly, this situation, before she broke down and did something really stupid, like cry and confess everything and anything. Tears already gathered behind her eyes.

"You're scared. Why? Have I harmed you?"

Xer's worry was very obvious, most notably in how he automatically stepped forward, arms opened as if to offer comfort. The one thing she didn't think she could handle was seeing a gentle caring side to him. She felt trapped when big hands securely held her upper arms and the thumbs stroked the soft flesh of her bare inner arm.

"Oh, no, no, you haven't hurt me. I just want to go home." She wished he wouldn't act this concerned, it felt too nice. His gentle touch coaxed her all-consuming hunger for a mate forward. The need to leave turned to desperation in her brain and left her anxious to get away. She didn't want to listen to her more lustful inclinations and push him to the floor, take his body, no matter how intriguing the notion may be.

"Then why are you scared?" Apparently he was still troubled by her apparent show of nerves, only now he seemed determined to get answers.

Sui was terrified, but there was no way she was going to answer his demand. It would open up issues she wasn't willing to tackle with him. Suddenly she found her saving grace in a less personal part of her life, but one just as important.

"I've acted most unprofessionally this evening and must leave before it goes any further." Truthfully, she did worry about how her actions in the hall would reflect on her full-time job. The speedball competition translator's post was only for the span of the contest. The company she worked for on a daily basis had lent her services out for the major event and in return received a great public relations boost. Without thinking twice, they could terminate her contract for the transgression. Although the fact she was only one of three who worked in the Zandian Communications department was on her side. She was their best translator, but that fact didn't make her irreplaceable.

"I've marked you and won't stand for your not being at my side, unless I choose otherwise." Xer crossed his arms over his muscular chest and made it apparent he'd no longer listen to her denials.

"You've got to be kidding me. No! For the last time I am an Earther, you can't mark me!"

That was it. She couldn't take it any more. Naked or not, she was leaving. Frantically she looked around the room and caught sight of her purse and clothes neatly stacked on a sideboard set back against a wall. Quickly she moved over and started grabbing up her clothes, putting on enough to be covered and started walking toward the door.

"Stop!"

Oh nuts, how could one word sound exactly like a royal command, one she didn't have the strength to deny. She turned around and looked at the most stubborn man known to exist. Okay, she had to think about what she was doing, because he was powerful and with a single word could send her back to home. Maybe it would be best if she didn't aggravate his anger.

"Yes, Your Royal Heir Apprentice?" Keeping her eyes down, she needed to regain some semblance of her composure, but was finding it very difficult to do.

"Don't bother to play the demure maiden with me. In case you haven't noticed, I can take, and rather enjoy, your sassy side." He stepped up, put his finger beneath her chin and lifted her face until their gazes met. "For now we'll agree to disagree on your origins. However, don't be foolish in thinking we won't readdress this issue later, because we most definitely will. In the meantime, you'll not contradict me when I say you're mine, marked and pleasured as such before witnesses."

The finger holding her chin up and intense brown eyes didn't lessen the meaning behind his words. If she blinked, he'd take it as though she accepted what he was saying. On the other hand, if she did nothing, she'd never get out of here.

"You may continue your duties as translator for Zandia in this speedball competition. However, you'll not evade your responsibilities to me, both personally and professionally. What I mean, specifically, is after each of our matches, you'll join me for dinner, dressed for my pleasure, and not leave my side until after the sun rises. And, most importantly, you'll continue to wear my mark." Xer was so close, and for many reasons she knew he shouldn't be able to turn her on, and yet Sui had to clench her legs tightly in a bid to lessen the need pulsing deep in her cleft.

She said nothing. There was no way she could agree to his conditions, and people didn't lie to their ruling family, even if they were denying their heritage.

"I'll not allow you to leave without your honored oath accepting to these terms."

"The mark, I don't..." Sui was about to claim her discomfort with its presence, only it wasn't true. She was enjoying the excitement spiraling around her body, the sense of anticipation of what was to come. What she'd not be able to handle was placing the jewel on herself. This was out of her comfort zone. "I'll not..."

"Enough!" The power of this man's presence didn't need a loud voice but when it rose, she jumped. "Give me your honored oath, now!"

"I promise on my honor, sir." In a quiet voice, she gave her promise, seeing it as the only way to be able to leave. She was surprised when he bent down and helped her put her shoes on.

Clasping her undergarments and purse close, she was surprised to have the prince on his knees helping her finish dressing. Once done, he stood, grasped her hand and made for the panel leading out to the hall's main entryway.

"Sir!" She was stunned. Prince Xer started striding bare assed naked out of the room and toward the front panel with her in tow.

Goodness gracious, please let there be no press about them. One digital image could bring about her downfall, and possibly cause him and Zandia a great deal of embarrassment, and she'd be the one to feel the backlash. "Please stop! You mustn't go out there naked."

Sui pleaded, tugged against his hand until he stopped and turned to look at her.

"What do you think you're doing!" She worked on tugging her hand free from his grip. No matter how much she fought for her freedom, he wasn't letting it go.

"Taking you home." The words were said on a matter-of-fact tone, albeit delivered by an impressive and aroused man. "And I told you to call me Xer."

"You can't go outside completely naked." Did he forget he wasn't wearing anything?

"Why not?"

"Gracious, this is Earth! Such an act would be insulting to your hosts." Was he crazy and the news hadn't made it this far away from home?

"Ah-ha! You said your hosts, and not my people, because you're Zandian." Arms crossed across his chest and a smile on his face said it all, he was rather proud and pleased with himself. Despite the upheaval, she was finding it hard not to laugh.

"Earth is your host and you said we'd agree to disagree. Now, please, Xer, I can make my own way home." It was difficult, but in order to come out on top, Sui needed to find her feet with this man.

"Don't ever insult me like that again." Xer closed the distance between them, stopping only when his hard body rested flush against her much smaller form. Tunneling his fingers through her hair, he held her skull carefully but tilted it up until they connected eye to eye. "Whether or not you're Zandian doesn't matter. Once I marked you, sweet baby girl, you became mine. Your pleasure is for me provide, as is every other need of yours, no matter how large or small. The most important role I now play in your life is to ensure your safety. I take all of this very seriously."

Oh boy, she was in even bigger trouble than she'd thought. How dare he go from being pigheaded and obstinate to thoughtful and loving in the blink of an eye? She felt it throughout her body when he'd called her "sweet baby girl". Again, her eyes began to tear, her heart already raced to a faster beat, and the pulses throbbed down between her legs to her pussy where honey once again gathered. If she wasn't careful, she'd be dropping at his feet and begging him to take her again and again.

"I need to go home." Sui moved her hands up to grasp his wrists and tugged. She had to get out of here.

"Don't be scared. I'm taking you home now." His voice was soft, soothing, and still seductive.

From out of nowhere, someone walked into her peripheral vision. Because she moved quickly, Xer never had a chance to stop her. She turned to face the intruder and cover the prince's nudity at the same time. In her subconscious, was also a need to protect him, from what she didn't know.

Once again, Rol calmly stood a few steps away, holding the black silk pants Xer had been wearing earlier.

The prince put his hands on her shoulders and squeezed. Pulling her back against him had his hard-on poking insistently at her back. Thankfully he said nothing about her actions, because she didn't think she could intelligently explain them away.

"Rol?"

After a moment of eye contact between the two men, which appeared to speak louder than words, and a final nod, the prince's second-in-command silently walked past the couple. He paused briefly to hand the garment to the prince before taking up his post at the front panel where he stood and waited.

A cool draft swept between them once Xer stepped back from her body and put his pants back on. Sui didn't turn around for one last look at his incredible cock. Her memories of the piece of flesh between his legs would have to hold her for a lifetime.

"Are you ready, Sui?" With an arm around her back, he waited until she nodded before he walked her out of the building, with Rol leading the way.

She actually felt sad. The evening had been eventful, and full of surprises, only now it was over. With her next breath

84

came the awareness of the sickening bundle called homesickness settling in her belly. Leaving this man and his reminders of home, good or bad, was something she hadn't expected to hurt this much or make her want things that weren't possible. All this brought to the forefront her desire for a truly imaginative lover who enjoyed her intelligence as well as her body. Someone who she turned on and, in return, made her want to fuck like a rabbit. Everything she could possibly want, just not with this man.

Once all three were settled into the back of the official transportation, the drive to her place was swift and silent. She gave herself a pep talk about not making any more waves. All she wanted to do was close the door on this evening as quickly as possible.

A few minutes later, the vehicle arrived at her building and parked in the no stopping zone. She didn't say anything when two men, who must be the prince's personal security, stepped out of the vehicle, and joined Sui, Xer and Rol as they walked into the lobby. It was late and the large communal space was empty except for the doorman.

Sui noticed one of the security men peeled off as the rest of the group moved en masse to the tube, but paid no attention to any of their actions. She was almost in the clear.

Chapter Nine

Pressing her hand to the front security plate, the lock popped and opened the main panel to her personal space. It wasn't large, but it was all hers. Stepping over the threshold, she turned and faced the three men remaining in the hallway. The security man who'd followed them up was turned around, busy checking the empty corridor. She spoke to the prince and his second-in-command.

"Thank you for seeing me home, Xer, Rol." Sui should have said something about enjoying the evening, but it was obvious to everyone she had and didn't need reiterating.

Taking her by surprise, both men stepped into the foyer, causing her to step back or be face to chest with a couple of half-naked men. Rol closed the panel behind them, moved into the living space and went straight to the large glass wall. Xer took her arm and brought her attention back to him.

She pokered right up. "I don't mean to be rude, but I'm tired. It's been an eventful day, and for me tomorrow starts early."

"Shhh, relax." He wrapped his arms around her and enveloped her, or as close as he could with her remaining clothes and purse clutched to her chest. "We'll sleep." Gentle kisses were dropped on the top of her head as his arms moved soothingly up and down her back. "Together."

If it were possible for her to stiffen even further, she did.

"No..."

"Yes, now go do whatever you need to before we all retire." After releasing and physically turning her to face the passageway. Xer gave her ass a double tap to get her moving.

Looking at him over her shoulder with disgust over his manhandling, she humphed and walked away from temptation and toward her wet room to clean up. Mindlessly she worked through her evening routine, steadfastly ignoring the presence of the two men in her living space.

"Retire?" Sui stopped scrubbing her face. Who says retire, wait a second, had he really said, "we all"? Because if he had, she was in more trouble than she thought. There was no more fight left in her—all her energy had been taken and left on the banquet table.

Stripping off her clothes, she put the items in the soiled clothing box in the corner of her room and entered the water closet to clean off. With the prince's sperm dried on her thighs, his scent covering her flesh, she realized one more thing. There was no desire in her to deny him anything. She wanted him to stay, forever, but it wouldn't do her any good to have those types of dreams. They weren't meant to come true.

Crap! It suddenly dawned on her, she may have given herself away for not being an Earther when she didn't demand protection from viruses and conception. Actually, having sex without a care before a room full of strangers who made a point of watching could also be a problem. She'd have to bluff her way out of that corner if it was ever used against her.

Using a soft sponge, she smoothed her favorite floral-scented soap over her breasts. The tips were tender from Xer's attentions. Their intimate time together had been completely unexpected and yet exactly how she'd always believed it should be. Zandians excelled in enjoying their bodies and the passionate play they were driven to express themselves through.

Rubbing the sponge down her belly to her mound, Sui came upon the mark the prince had placed on her. It was a beautiful piece of jewelry. Black and aquamarine, she knew these two colors officially labeled something as belonging to the Roiroirepus clan. They also happened to look perfect on her, they stood out against her smooth, white flesh. Her clit was still firm with the hook holding it in a continual state of need. The beaded fringe leading to the bullet comfortably settled in her back passage nudged her desire even higher, still bringing mini, pulsating beats rushing through her cleft as if searching for fulfillment.

She enjoyed the beauty of the mark as a unique piece of jewelry, however, remembering the ceremony leading up to its placement brought a warm glow spreading through her body. With a jaw-cracking yawn, she decided to leave it on until she rose in the morning for work. Using the sponge, Sui quickly finished washing and stepped out to stand before the dry wall. With blasts of warm air hitting her, little time passed before she was dry and feeling her exhaustion.

Tears were once again building behind her eyes. This evening she'd felt closer to Zandia than she had since her parents had left. It left her with a variety of emotions running loose throughout her, each more fascinating than the last. Besides the homesickness, she was most shocked by a fresh sense of her own physical appeal to others. The new experience of being desirous to a Zandian wasn't something she'd thought to ever feel. Sui knew in her heart of hearts her appearance would gain her no attention back home, other than maybe looks of distaste, but definitely not admiration, or lust like she'd enjoyed tonight.

Sad, tired, and surprised because she was still horny, the decision to go to sleep before she did something she'd later regret had her slipping on a light sleep shift. Turning off the light, Sui left the wet room and headed into her sleeping area.

There was no hope tonight of staving off Somnus' call, she was too exhausted. Sitting on the soft mattress, she curled onto her side and pulled the thin blanket over her shoulders. Within minutes, she was tiptoeing blissfully through the land of slumber.

ೞೞೞ

"Isn't she the most beautiful woman you've ever seen?" Xer stood beside the bed looking down at the young and vulnerable petite blonde. "Those silky curls around her head are intoxicating and the delicate pelt between her legs is enthralling."

"I knew with one look at her you'd want your dick embedded in her lush clasp."

"Tell me." Xer whispered so as not to disturb the sleeping beauty. Thankfully the other man knew what he was looking for, his take on the woman sleeping before them.

"She calls herself an Earther and yet, at the same time, doesn't deny she's Zandian." The tall, bald and powerful second-in-command's frown showed he too felt they were missing something obvious.

"Semantics." Xer shrugged off the finding.

"No, I think she's being very careful about something but can't go so far as to deny her true heritage," he continued as he moved to stand next to his friend. "It's an odd mix I see. She appears fiercely independent in nature, and if I didn't know better, I'd say Sui Erom had been educated through the

Zandian universal relations path. Manners and linguistic abilities say as much, but she lost it when I took her to the seamstress for proper clothes. She was mad and said she wouldn't wear something that bared her body."

"It would be a shame to hide this stunning feminine form. She seemed fine during the marking ceremony." Confused, Xer looked over at his friend for clarification. He'd been so deeply lost in his passion during the ritual he now feared he'd missed something important.

"And that's exactly what's been driving me nuts. It was peculiar how she went from wanting to cover herself like a typical Earther to lustfully riding your cock before a roomful of strangers. This petite female wallowed in the passion you created together, and didn't shy away from its power." Rol's bewilderment was obvious.

"Don't ask me to prove this but I know she is Zandian." Adamant in his blind belief in her heritage, the prince now needed to decide why it mattered this much. There was much to think through in regards to this situation, it had all happened so quickly he'd blindly gone where he felt he should. However, he was sure there was more between him and Sui than the marking, only he didn't have it all figured out yet. Shoot, in his lifetime there'd been no other person able to twist him around their will as much as this pretty little woman had done in one day.

"There's more than pride in having marked her, isn't there?"

"Yes, although I'm not entirely sure what else it is, but whatever it is, it's waiting for me to seize it." As he spoke, he watched her in peaceful repose, gently stroking a finger over her soft cheek. "Are the guards in place?"

"They are, although this building is nowhere near being a secured site for you to spend much time in," Rol stated.

"If this is where she sleeps, then this is where I'll be." He dropped his pants and left them there on the floor. Moving to the other side, he pushed the blanket down to her feet with the thought of how he'd ensure her comfort, keep her warm while she slept.

Lying down, he was ready to spoon his chest to her back, his groin to her luscious ass, his strong legs, from thigh to toe, to rest against her soft feminine form. The need to press his flesh to hers had him bracing himself on one arm and taking in the basic white shift she wore. Sui continued to surprise him. The simplicity of her gown was somehow as seductive as her dress this evening had been. Six Turns to Love—it was something he'd have to make sure she wore again. He'd enjoyed unwrapping her.

He lifted the bottom edge of the short gown and was pleased to see she hadn't taken his mark off. Xer looked to his friend for help and they carefully disrobed her, not waking her from the deep sleep she'd fallen into.

"Look, she kept my mark on." Proud, he whispered to Rol without taking his gaze from the lush beauty beside him.

Stroking a hand over her smooth round ass, enjoying the connection to her through touch was surprisingly satisfying. Sexually, women had been a part of his life since his thirteenth year, but never had he felt linked with one outside of fucking. The need he felt to protect and cosset was strong with Sui.

"So silky and soft, I could spend hours touching her supple skin. Did you ever think you'd find a woman with such an unusual appearance to be this stunning and perfect?" Awe joined his jumbled emotions and the wonderful petite woman beside him remained oblivious.

There'd been other women who had the grabbed-by-the-balls kind of effect on him, but once he'd fucked them, there'd been little else to hold his attention. However, this tiny woman had stayed in his thoughts since first hearing her voice resonate throughout the arena. When he'd seen her, Xer had thought his cock would embarrass him and come right there. The torture had continued because next was the best sex he'd ever experienced, and not one hour later, he was still hard and eager to enjoy more of her moist pussy. But he wouldn't because she was unsettled with the situation.

"You can't share her, can you?" There was a surprised tone in Rol's voice. Having grown up together, this was a first for the prince. Never before had the issue of sharing been questioned, especially in regards to his best friend.

Xer's hand strayed over her hip, into the dip of her waist before it slid farther down to rest over her belly. Unable to help himself, he teased the tip of his little finger in, out and around the bellybutton. She squirmed a little, settling deeper into his grasp.

"No, right now I don't think I can." An aura of possession surrounded him and a sense of vulnerability he didn't particularly like. Xer was ready to fight for clarity of what was between them. He had to accept it would come at some point, but not now.

Dropping little kisses along her shoulder, he pulled her closer to him, enjoying the moment of peace. A soft natural scent had settled in the hollow of her neck. His nose nudged in, moving along the tantalizing path, inhaling and enjoying Sui.

As his nose moved closer to its goal, the delicate pink lobe resting at the bottom of her ear, he left gentle kisses along her hairline and then he stopped.

Stunned, he jerked up to rest on his knees behind her. With mouth agape and eyes wide open, he used his fingers to smooth her tresses away from her ear and unearthed proof of her true nationality.

The little blonde was chipped! On the first day at a Zandian educational facility all new entrants were separated by gender and fixed with a permanent virus-free chip behind their left ear. Whenever a new virus was discovered and an antidote developed, the chips were updated. And there, beneath the chip, was an implanted infertility device.

"Look, Rol. See, Sui Erom is Zandian!" Looking up at his friend, Xer whispered with all the self-righteousness he felt was deserved. "We must find her fold, search for any missing women. Her paternal moniker must be Erom. Ensure all of this lines fold leaders are located and asked to account for their women. I must know why she's here, claiming to be an Earther."

Determination, and some anger, had him not wanting to wait until dawn for answers. How dare some fold leader allow a young female under their control to exist on her own? The more he thought about it, the angrier he became. Sui could've been in trouble, harmed, even killed, and there was no one here for her to turn to for help.

"I'll go out to the living space, find someone to bring me a commo-box now, and start sending directives back to Zandia. We'll get answers, Xer." Rol was in his element, solving problems, ensuring his friend was safe and in a good place to rule with all the energy and intelligence he possessed.

"Until we have definitive news from Zandia, we say nothing to Sui." For the time being, he'd said all he would on the subject and had already moved his attention back to the sleeping woman.

Gently he eased her onto her back, leaving her fully exposed before the two men and set out to indulge his rising needs.

"Sui, my beauty, I will cherish you as no other man ever has before," he whispered as he stroked his hand down to cup her pussy in ownership.

Putting his other hand under her head, he lifted her up to meet him, lips to lips, and kissed her with all the wild and untamed emotions racing through him and into her.

Chapter Ten

"Xer!"

Sui woke calling out his name and he was thrilled to hear it burst from her lips. As a reward, he leaned over and ravished her soft tempting mouth.

Her plump red lips, still looking tender from their earlier loving, were now eagerly reaching upwards to meet his. There was no gentling her into the moment. She took his kiss, accepted the hard press of his mouth, the thrust of his tongue, and she gave him her groans of ecstasy by return. Like an explosion, his passion heated up even further when she trusted him to hold her weight by lifting her arms and wrapping them around his neck. She held him close, instantly submitting to the pleasure he offered.

Wanting to slow things down, Xer lowered her body and started circling her slit's opening with a single digit, wringing gasps of need from her. Occasionally his finger would make a foray up and around her captive, bejeweled clit, spreading her honey, but only enough to keep her wanting more.

"How do you do this?"

While her hand stroked over his bare flesh, he enjoyed the feel of her soft form against his. Looking into her eyes, he could see she was quickly sinking into the lust he created, but as yet her mind hadn't completely fallen under the erotic spell he wove.

"Do what, sweet petite? You have needs and, as they should, they respond to me, the man whose mark you wear." In no way was he going to allow her to forget how her desires were his to indulge, his to drive higher and quench.

"Ohhh..." Xer got off on seeing how Sui couldn't hold back her vocal appreciation for the slow and seductive presence he was sending in between her lower lips. He stirred up her sleek nectar coated slit before pulling his finger free, only to start over again.

"Spread your legs for me, love, let me see those lovely pink puffy lips surrounding my finger." His gaze moved from hers down to her bountiful breasts and took in the tight pink nipples, pointing up and looking eager for attention. He slipped his gaze farther down, over her belly to her small blonde pelt pointing to her nub. Black onyx hook and beads led his gaze directly to her slit.

"Ungh, the onyx..."

Perfect. When she moved her legs, the stone bullet obviously made itself known in her back passage and seemed to tempt her needs. Both her hands fell back to rest on the pillow beside her head. In the moment of surrender, she looked wonderful, very seductive, and all his.

"Ahhh, now you remember the solid presence still resting in your tight ass. Do you feel its unrelenting presence?" There was a struggle going on within himself to drag his gaze away from his busy finger. He wanted to see her face, flush with pleasure as much as he needed to watch his possession of her pussy.

"Yes," she whispered while looking up at him.

Sui looked tired, smudges under her eyes, and yet he felt a driving need to possess her body and soul, especially since he'd discovered she was truly Zandian. She'd been right. An Earther couldn't be held by the marking tradition, but a Zandian could. He needed to ensure she knew from this moment onwards she belonged to him, no matter what.

"I know you're tired and must be tender from earlier, but can you take me once more?" Xer asked her softly, as his finger continued to slowly fuck in and out of her moistening pussy.

"Please, yes, please ease this ache you've created." She sounded exhausted but her needs were raging. There'd be no sleep until they were satisfied, he'd make sure of that.

"It's because you inspire me and my lust to seek out even more from you and your luscious body." As he spoke, his gaze moved back to his hand between her spread legs.

Each time his single digit pulled free of her pussy's clench, he saw how it was slick with honey. He was caught in a wicked trap and couldn't look away from his finger fucking in and out of her dripping slit, teasing the sugared walls with a curled finger dragging here and there along the way.

Her hips tried to bump up against his hand, but her position didn't allow for easy movement. Sui reached down and held his hand, pressed it closer to her cleft, burying the finger as deep as it could go. When apparently one wasn't enough, she pushed another digit in and held them inside with a firm grip on his wrist.

Xer was used to women following his direction to find their orgasms. A woman taking what she needed was different, and he liked it very much when this woman took her desire in hand and found her peak.

He held her gaze as she slowly moved the duo in and out, grinding his palm against her mound and excited nub. She licked her lips and he struggled not to pull his hand away and replace it with his hard cock, riding her into climaxing.

She glowed with power and he was instantly addicted to the intoxicated feeling she was giving him. Sui was a strong confident woman, comfortable in her sensual self, and her ability to take him to unbelievable passionate heights. His dick stiffened even further when she came by using his hand.

As he gloried in feeling her pulsate around him, he knew without a doubt, she was his woman.

"You are so beautiful, Sui. It was such a turn on to see you take my hand and use it to find your release."

When she moved his fingers and scraped them along the beaded fringe of his mark, it was more than he could take. Settling on his knees beside her body, he was hard-pressed not to move back between her legs and fuck her till they both came. Instead, he wanted to keep things slow and moved his free hand to stroke his hard cock.

"You're incredibly sexy."

"You were teasing me, and I couldn't take it any longer." She panted and he thrived seeing her struggle against the passion still possessing her body.

"Put your hand on your breast, sweet petite. Pinch one of those tight nipples begging for attention." Xer kept stroking his cock slowly. Loving this woman should never be rushed, even though watching her, touching her, put a big strain on his control.

All those beliefs flew out the window when her delicate fingers tweaked the pointed tip hard, pulled and twisted, groaning as she lost herself once again in the erotic waves rushing through her body.

"Oh yes..." Still firmly holding his wrist, she used the palm of his hand to grind and tease her clit, pressing it harder and harder before using her grip on him to thrust his fingers in and out of her pussy at a faster rate.

"You're so wet, lush…" His gaze danced back and forth between where she was once again using his hand as a fuck toy, to where her large breasts were being pinched and pulled by her tiny fingers, and her face. Pleasure painted her features with a flush, brightest on her cheeks, and was utterly enticing. Sui's open mouth and half-mast, glazed-over blue eyes was almost more than he could take. Pulling his hand from his cock, he dipped a finger between her parted lips and teased her tongue. She surprised him by closing her mouth around the digit and used her tongue to lovingly search for his essence before he took it out and painted the moisture over the forgotten nipple.

"Oh! Oh! Xer!" Holding his hand pressed hard against her pussy and mound, she arched her back enough to bring her breasts up for more attention from his fingers. And again she climaxed chanting his name.

It was difficult to hold still but he did and enjoyed how she fell apart around him. His fingers were squeezed, pulled and treated to the most erotic massage they'd ever experienced. The desire to thrust his cock in and out of the pulsating wet wonderland was all consuming.

He looked on as she slowly came back to herself, and it was an eye-opening experience. When her arms, as if boneless, flopped down to her sides, she looked up at him and blushed.

"How could it be possible, after one of the most erotic moments of my life, you still look young, fresh, untouched?" Xer was no longer surprised at the desire she built within him.

With his fingers buried in her dripping slit, he scissored them and followed up with a gentle thrust and retreat before he pulled them free, and saw the digits were covered in cream. He lifted them up to his mouth and watched her face redden further as he sucked them clean, savoring her essence.

"Uh! What are you doing?"

"Hmmm, you taste delicious. I'm too anxious to bury my cock in this pussy otherwise I'd eat you up, but that will have to wait. Right now I want to take you even further down the path to pleasure we've been on. I want to make you scream as you come on my dick." Crawling over to rest between her now limp legs, he lodged the weeping crown of his cock into her moist warm opening.

Hooking her legs over the crook in his arms, Xer rose up onto his knees and started to slowly nudge a portion of his rod in and out of her lush paradise. He found it difficult to hold back his need to go wild, but he felt for now he must.

He made no pretense of looking anywhere other than where they were connected. His cock was ready to ravage her delicate pink folds. He fought to keep it slow, build her lust back up, although he already felt the walls of her pussy grab at him, fight to keep him inside. Little by little, he added more of his cock until he bottomed out, but continued to keep the motion slow and evenly paced. Each time he glided in and out of her, the mark's fringe rubbed along his length, it felt like her fingers were tapping along his dick.

"Ohhh, I can feel all of you, every solid inch sliding in and out of me." Both her hands moved up and over her belly, then stroked up to cup her breasts.

"How do you like my mark?" He leaned forward, now resting his hands on either side of her shoulders, and held his cock fully seated in her slit, nudging for that last little bit of space.

He bent her in half taking advantage of the opportunity to kiss her softly. He lingered over the kiss, letting her search for her true answer to his query before voicing it. The tip of his tongue snaked along the slightly parted seam, darting in here, dropping a small bussing kiss there.

His need rose higher through each groan his kisses and possession of her body created, giving his rod an even greater desire to come, but he wanted to hear her words first.

"Tell me, my petite, how does my mark feel in your ass as my cock fills your lush pussy?" He pulled back from the temptation her lips posed and moved to her left, taking a bite of her ear lobe. There was no doubt she was completely lost in the sensual pool they'd created together, because there wasn't a flinch or tensing of her body in fear of him discovering the chip, something that marked her true origins.

Small soft hands moved up and stroked his smooth head, her delicate fingers teased his senses to further action. He nibbled on her ear a little more firmly, and her arms fell and wrapped around his neck. Sui turned her head giving him better access to her neck.

"You...complete...me."

Those three words broke him and his much lauded hold over his passion.

One at a time he moved his arms, settling down onto his forearms, releasing each of her legs from their confinement.

"I'm sorry..." was all he could manage before he started to thrust his cock in and out of her damp clutches.

"Xer?" He heard her confusion over his odd apology but couldn't stop fucking to explain.

Faster, harder, each stroke more powerful than the last. He stabbed into her pussy, needing to feel her surrounding his cock. It became more difficult to pull himself free of her squeezing slit, but he managed, bouncing his balls off her ass with each returning plunge.

"...sorry..." Xer was ready to come but he squeezed every muscle, forced his thoughts to more mundane matters all in a bid to stave off his climax until she came.

She moved her legs, pressing her bare feet against his hips, giving him an infinitesimal amount of space to sink into her heated depths that much farther than before. He was set adrift on the waves of his lust.

"...ah shit..."

"Xer!"

"...mine..."

Focused entirely on reaching the pinnacle of pleasure, he took them both higher and higher with each forceful thrust by his hard, unyielding dick into her, wet, clinging slit.

"Oh yes, yes, Xer..."

"Come for me, Sui, come for me now."

Desperation had him as close to begging as he'd ever been before.

"Ahhh!" Her pussy pulsed and squeezed over and over again as she screamed as she came, pulling him over the wall with her.

"Fuck!" The cum rose from his soul up to his balls and shot out the end of his cock, splashing time and again in her deepest reaches. He pushed deeper still. Something inside him wouldn't rest until he'd deposited his seed well within her welcoming warmth.

Soft, supple legs moved to wrap around his waist, and held him close. He loved every moment spent there.

"I love the feel of your cock pulsating inside me." She whispered in his ear while she rubbed his shiny dome.

Carefully he threaded his fingers through her silken locks and kissed her, softly at first, then he allowed the wild feelings still racing through him to come to the surface. All the while he continued to move his satisfied cock in small strokes. He never wanted to leave her warm, wet depths.

After a few moments of gently loving her, he took her lower lip in between his front teeth and tugged. The act brought her eyes open, barely, and although unfocused, they rested on him. Releasing her plump flesh, he took a moment to soothe the skin with his tongue before he spoke as if making a royal decree this time, there'd be no objections accepted.

"You're mine, Sui Erom!" He wanted, no needed, her to understand how serious he was about her.

"Of course I am, Xer." Her hands caressed his head as she spoke, exhaustion slurring her words. "Of course I am. For now, I'm yours." Lids slowly lowered over blue orbs, and she was asleep before he'd pulled fully free of her warmth.

"No, my sweet petite, forever mine." He dropped a kiss on her lips and moved up to his knees between her thighs. Of their own volition, his eyes dropped to watch his cum slip from her pussy. There was no way he'd ever let her out of his life.

Chapter Eleven

Dawn was ready to break across the city when Sui opened her eyes. Blinking, she focused on the wall where the time was projected. My goodness, not even five and she was awake. It was an obscene hour, and one she wouldn't normally be up to greet. Her mind spun and searched for a reason why today she did.

Awareness slowly filtered through her when she felt the large solid presence behind her, heat radiating over her body in waves. She looked down to see a smooth, muscular arm resting over her waist, and a hand grasping hold of her breast. Bare powerful legs pressed against hers and a large erect cock had wedged itself in her crease with the head pushing between her thighs.

Not sure if she tensed up because she knew who it was or because he'd had the guts to stay after saying he was sorry while he took her body and soul to nirvana. After being more delectably possessive and loving than she'd ever dreamt possible while he fucked her senseless, he'd ruined it all with an apology.

On one side of her mind there was wishful thinking to have such a man want her by his side. On the other, it was her worst nightmare. Nothing good could come from getting attached to Xer, a Zandian and heir to the throne.

Reality crashed in on her with a silent snigger. When had her ego become this large? It was ridiculous to think she could hold such a handsome and powerful man. He'd merely wanted sex, which had been fine with her.

Slowly she inched away from his intoxicating warmth and off the bed. Stepping away from the edge of the cushioned platform, she looked at him—really looked—and was surprised to find he looked so young. In his sleep there was a sense of peace about him, like this was the only time he stopped moving, going, doing.

Sui quietly moved about her room before going into the wet room. Since she was up, she might as well get dressed and go into work early. There'd been a stack of work on her desk before she'd made her first appearance as an official translator at the competition. It was an easy decision to go in and try to make a dent in the translations before going back to the stadium this evening.

Besides, it was better than staying and having an awkward moment with the prince in broad daylight. She doubted he'd feel uncomfortable; she was sure this type of situation was too common for it to disturb Xer. But it would be for her.

Going about her morning preparations gave Sui too much time to think and second-guess her actions, and the motivations behind them. At no point in her life had she felt complete, and yet there was also no point in counting on the feeling continuing.

Standing in the water closet, cleaning off the spendings from their late night play, she couldn't ignore the mark hooked around her clit and running along to where it was still buried in her ass. For some reason she wasn't entirely sure of what to do, it felt wrong to take it off. Even after her body had been fully satisfied, her clit remained firm with the slim wire pinching it.

The beaded fringe settled between her thighs had repeatedly sent erotic pulses throughout her body each time she moved a muscle.

For her peace of mind, she finally acknowledged it would be best for all concerned if she made herself available for the prince as long as the Zandian entourage was on Earth. With a smile, she told herself if he wanted more from her, then she'd go with it and enjoy every moment until they left. Their time together was quickly becoming everything her dreams were made of.

Finished dressing for the day, she walked back into the sleeping area and took one last look at the bed and the man lying naked in the center, now sprawled out with muscled limbs pointing to the four corners. What an incredibly sexy sight he presented, and she admitted, this was a spectacular way to begin any day.

The determined will she possessed to fight for her freedom was stronger than ever, but looking at this man, she knew it would be next to impossible to deny him anything.

Taking a deep breath full of regret, she walked out to the living room and was quickly brought up short by Rol standing in all his powerful nakedness in the living space looking out the glass wall.

He didn't turn around to look at her but Sui could tell he was aware of her standing there. The man was an impressive-looking specimen, with flawless smooth buns of steel that looked very strokable. Obviously he'd made himself at home because he was holding a staple Earther item, particularly a favorite of the American sector she resided in—a hot steaming cup of black mort.

It wasn't to her particular tastes for a morning beverage, but she liked trying new things and this had been something she'd never seen on Zandia. Even more important to her than the taste was being able to talk at work about things other people enjoyed. It was part of socializing and fitting in, so she drank it.

"He cares for you," Rol rumbled out, still not facing her.

"Pardon me?" She was confused. This was the sexiest playboy of the Universe they were talking about, not your average man.

"You are the first woman he's ever marked. Xer has never cared to tie a female this firmly to his side before he heard your voice." Turning around, he looked at her.

"Oh please, I'm not stupid. The man has now, and has had in the past, more women than anyone alive." Sui wasn't aware her fire and spirit were showing instead of the convivial hostess she'd been careful to show them previously. "Besides, how can someone care enough to apply a mark before even having met the person, much less spoken to them?"

"Don't play games with me, Sui. What I'm doing here is giving you fair warning. Xer cares, more than I've seen him ever express before."

There was no anger or disgust lacing his words, but at the same time, what he was saying wasn't something she wanted to hear.

"No, no, this is not happening to me. You're wrong." She shook her head. There was no way this was happening to her. Life here on Earth, in the American sector, had been exactly what she wanted. She was happy here and fulfilled in ways that would never have been possible back home. "Last night he said he was sorry to take me, that doesn't sound like a man who cares."

"Nevertheless, I'm right. From our baby beds, we've been friends, we've grown into manhood together. I know him better than anyone else." He put the cup down and walked over to stand in front of her. Gently he grasped her upper arms, looked intently into her eyes and continued, "Yes, he's a strong confident man, but he's just that, a man who has feelings. And this is one he's never experienced before. All I'm saying is be prepared for anything, because he cares."

Needing to regroup, she pulled back and quickly made her way to the front panel. Going to work was what she needed to do. Something else to focus on other than the man lying naked on her bed in the other room, or the words coming from his friend's mouth.

"Security will be there to protect you. Don't try to loose them or stop them from doing their job."

She appreciated him telling her the truth instead of having her be spooked. However, after the brief show of temper, she hoped Rol could see she wasn't easily scared. Sui thought it was obvious she'd been shaken by what he had to say and she couldn't let it happen again, she needed to be on her toes with these guys.

The little blonde beauty before him looked rebellious, ready to argue with his order, and he couldn't blame her. The air around them turned thick with the tension. Without taking his gaze from her, he watched her rigid back, and waited for her to respond. After a long minute of silence, and without turning around, Sui silently gave him her nod of acceptance and left.

Rol had taken a risk in warning her, but somehow he felt in the future she'd need someone guaranteed to give her a straightforward and honest answer and he'd be there to do it. To him the future was clear. At the end of the speedball competition, Sui Erom would be returning to Zandia with them.

And that, amongst other things, would throw her into the deep end of a life she hasn't been prepared for. She'll need friends.

Walking back to the hot drink he'd put down earlier, he slowly finished it off. All night he'd been working the commo-box looking for answers and what he'd found thus far was going to surprise Xer as much as it had him. Taking a few moments to compose himself, he took in the sights spread out before him in the early pink sunrise.

Both sadness and excitement mixed quietly together within his soul. No part of his existence would be left untouched by these events. As of right now, Rol didn't think Sui had accepted the change her life was going to take. He wasn't entirely sure Xer had either, but thought his friend was more open to the new path emerging before him than she was. No matter what, Rol would be there to support him, them, all the way.

It wasn't going to be easy for anyone, but their coming together held such unimaginable promise. Personally he was eager to have it begin.

"Sui!"

With a twitch of a smile, he turned toward the opening leading into the sleeping area and waited for his friend to burst forth looking for the woman whose independent nature was going to throw him into a fit.

"Sui! Where are..." In such a small space, his voice reverberated off the walls, but it was obvious he didn't care who might hear his call as long as it was the woman he sought.

"She's already left for work." Holding up his hand to stave off the expected question, Rol answered before it was asked. "Yes, I arranged for a security detail to accompany her, and yes, they each have a commo-box on them. Use nine if you need to reach Sui. It's been keyed in for those on her particular detail."

"Shit! I never heard her get up." Rubbing a hand down his face, Xer looked around and took a minute to see how she chose to live down here on Earth. Moving to sit on the stuffed bench, he found himself surprised, there was a real sense of comfort radiating about the place.

"It's a very peaceful setting, soothing, which isn't something I equate with this planet." He searched out details, anything to give him more information about the woman who lived here and why she was denying her heritage. Finally he asked his friend the one question resting most heavily on his mind. "What have you found out?"

Rol returned to the living space with two hot cups of black mort. First, he handed one to his friend before he moved back to stand at the picture glass.

"No report for a missing Sui Erom has been posted, nor is there a birth record for one. There are two dozen Erom folds. Thus far all but three have been cleared." He took another sip of the hot drink.

"Hmmm, she's changed her moniker. Search for every female child born between twenty and twenty-five years ago with Sui on their identity documentation. At the same time, and using the same parameters, start a fold search. The latter will take longer but it may catch either an unofficial or a paternal requested change."

"Done." Rol watched his friend take his first sip from the cup.

"What is this shit?"

"Apparently an American sector basic energy source."

"Tastes like poison." Xer was far from being impressed with the black mort, but went back for another taste.

"Yes, a burnt beverage, but I acquired a yen for it about four hours ago and have been steadily sucking it down ever since. Besides, there's nothing in the Universe like our tekor juice to give you an energy boost, be healthy and taste good at the same time."

"Rol, why do you think she didn't wake me up?" There was an infinitesimal hint of insecurity in his query and he didn't like it one bit.

"She's scared. I'm not sure why, but I see an incredible amount of fear swirling about her. And no, I don't believe she's afraid you'll harm her but something else. You have to speak to her about it though. How about if you ask her out on the American sector mainstay, a date? Talk about what's on her mind, get to know her, reassure her, but only if you want to keep her. If you don't, then leave her be."

"Yes, I'm keeping her. No matter what Sui may think, she'll be returning to Zandia with us." Emphatic about his decision, he stood and walked the room, taking in the smallest of details, wondering what it might tell him about Sui. "But first I must get her to trust me, and I think your date idea is the best solution. After our match tonight will be the perfect time."

Cℨℰℬℵℬ

"*Buzz.* Sui Erom has a guest waiting in reception zone three."

Stopping her current translation was easy. It was a letter of dry drivel from a man wanting to sell his colonic treatment on Zandia. His application was riddled with problems and inappropriate language, something she knew wouldn't be appreciated at the consumer products bureau on her home planet.

Sui's mood wasn't helped by the mark's presence. It was driving her nuts, actually she was finding it difficult to focus on anything other than her body's rising demand for satisfaction.

She wasn't expecting a visitor but a break would be appreciated. As she walked down the hallway, the fringe from Xer's mark madly tickled at her thighs. Moving toward the visitor's reception room, she was brought up short by the sight of a member of His Royal Heir Apprentice's security team. The man who'd been her shadow since leaving home this morning stopped behind her, obviously nodding to the other man who opened the panel for her to enter.

Great, Xer and the emotions he created in her were not something she felt capable of handling right now, not at work, or any time soon. And most especially not with her body screaming with pleasure from his mark.

Luck wasn't on her side. Taking a deep breath, she stepped into the room and found herself facing the future king of Zandia, and the man who had rocked her body with more orgasms than she'd ever thought possible.

Before the panel closed behind her, she dropped to the floor and greet the prince formally. Legs pressed close together, she sank to her knees, laid her chest and forehead to the ground before his feet with arms spread wide out to the sides. Not wearing the Six Turns to Love made this move much easier this time around, wearing his mark added other problems.

"Good wishes to you my sweet petite." Reaching down, he grasped hold of her upper arms and helped her stand. "Please, no more formal greetings between us. Now rise and give me a kiss."

As soon as she was on her feet, Xer pulled her into his embrace, held her close and dropped soft kisses on her lips. He whispered for her alone to hear, "Do you still wear my mark?"

After a small nod, he deepened the kiss even further while gripping her rear cheeks.

"When the match ends tonight, will you join me for dinner? I mean, will you accompany me on an American sector-style date?"

There was a note of uncertainty in his words, she found it endearing, and figured she must've imagined it.

"Oh, I'm not sure. After working all day today, very little slee—"

"You have to eat."

"Yes, but—"

"Then it's all settled. Once the game is finished, you'll wait for me to collect you from your booth." Giving her a quick squeeze and tap to her rear, he started to leave.

Turning at the opened panel, he gave one last demand over his shoulder before leaving. "And do something about your voice, it's too sexy and distracts the team."

Chapter Twelve

"That is a full stop match for the Zandian Zoolopeans and Pelokian Partillerans. The reigning speedball champion Zoolopeans won with a score of eight holes to six." Sui waited for her next turn while the other language interpreters ran through their translations.

There was a timeline variation they all worked on, arranged and agreed between them before each match started. Some languages, like Pelokian, based entirely on clucking sounds, took much longer to speak than standard English or Zandian.

"Lead scorer for the match, and the overall high scorer for the competition thus far, is captain of the Zandian Zoolopeans, number fifteen, His Royal Heir Apprentice, Prince Xer III..."

Sui knew there was a smile in her voice and professionalism demanded she work harder to hold it back, but inside she was very proud of him and all the Zoolopeans. It'd been funny, his demand she change her voice. The man had looked very determined she do this and yet he had to know it wasn't possible. How she sounded was something she had no control over. She was born with the voice and there was nothing she could do to alter it. Besides, he was all she'd thought about today. No matter how many times they had sex, she still wanted more.

To bad if he was turned on when her voice came out over the arena's sound system. It was only fair considering her current condition. Watching him run up and down the court in his skin suit while she sat up in the booth wearing his mark had kept her hot and bothered for the entire match. Concentration was difficult for her to grasp right now. He could deal with her voice if she could handle her rising lust.

"As reigning champions, they've won the two required matches to automatically advance on to the quarter-finals."

Great, more games to call, more time spent with the gorgeous hunk, and more heartbreak coming her way when it was all over. In the end, Sui was sure all the pain would be worth every glorious sensual minute she'd experienced in his arms.

After completing her paperwork, she touched the sound plug in her ear and signed off with her supervisor, the last step in closing down the booth communication system. Sui collected her personal belongings, looked toward her shadow for the day and left the room, heading down to sign out of the arena. As she had for the past few days, she walked down the long hallway, making her way to the tube, only to be hit by the lowest point in her day.

"Stop! Royal Mark, you must go no further," the man shouted, despite there being no need. The hall was empty, allowing his words to echo off the walls, floor, and throughout her being.

With a frown on her face, she determinedly continued onwards. She had a name—it was Sui Erom, not Royal Mark. Tears began to build in her eyes. The way women were treated as property was one of the things she hated most about Zandia. Purposely she ignored the man and kept moving steadily forward with her dignity wrapped closely around her.

"Stop, I say!"

Heavy footsteps could be heard rushing up behind her but she wouldn't stop, nor would she acknowledge anyone calling her by anything other than her name. She kept her watered gaze down on the floor, and by shear will alone she kept moving forward.

"You must stop, Royal Mark, we are to wa—"

Before the guard touched her, Sui walked right into a solid, unforgiving wall. Blinking, she focused her teary gaze and found herself looking into the most incredible brown eyes she'd ever seen.

Xer's.

She wasn't sure why, but his presence felt comforting, protective, and her tears freely fell down her cheeks. Allowing her forehead to rest against his chest, she silently cried, sighing deeply when he put his arms around her and carefully held her close.

"Shhh, it's all right, baby girl." Big rough hands rubbed soothingly up and down her back. "Everything is fine. Now relax, take a deep breath and tell me what's the matter. Why didn't you wait for me?"

Shaking her head, she sniffled and tried to rein in her out of control emotions. She'd forgotten she was supposed to wait for him.

Xer looked over her head at the man behind her, demanding an answer for why Sui was upset.

"The Royal Mark was—" The guard started to explain only to be cut off by the prince.

"Her name is Sui." The statement was offered not in anger or as a demand, but merely as fact. Her tears started to fall in earnest, now not so silently.

"Okay, okay..." He patted her on the back, unsure what to do with the quickly disintegrating situation. Looking from the security guard, her personal guard, to Rol for help, he received none. His friend seemed as confused as he was.

Not sure how best to handle her tears, he decided to take her away from whatever had obviously upset her and put it to rights.

With no effort, he picked her up, holding her close to his chest, and made his way back to the secured tube he'd taken to her floor from the player level. After Rol and their guards stepped in, they went back down, going twelve levels in less time than it took to blink an eye. Her tears dampened his neck and her cries, albeit quieter, still filled the quiet void of the moving tube.

"All's well, little one, don't cry." He meant it, the sound of her tears was painful to more than his ears, they tore at his heart.

Once the door to the tube opened, Xer made his way through various corridors, twisting this way and that before finally making it out to his waiting vehicle. Having collected more personnel along the way, it was quickly becoming a crowd. They all squished into the transportation and were on the road a few minutes before he lost the tight grip on his patience.

"That's it!" Sui was still leaking water from her eyes, people surrounded them and he felt his priority was to soothe the woman in his arms, quickly. "Stop! I said stop this vehicle! Now everybody get out. Yes, Rol, you as well."

"We can't leave you—" With concern, his friend started to dictate the necessity of keeping him secure, especially in an unknown section of the strange big and bustling city.

Xer knew it was a relatively peaceful place but he was a member of the Zandian ruling clan and had enemies always looking for an opportunity to do away with him. However, this issue with Sui was important and had to be handled.

"Now, Rol! I want a few moments alone with Sui, nothing more." Burying his fingers through her curls, rubbing his nose along the soft slope of her cheek, he whispered nonsense into her ear before he spoke to his second-in-command one last time. "Just a few minutes on our own, okay?"

"Fine. A man will be on each entry point, as well as one in front and another behind. But I'll stay here. I don't like this at all, it's very dangerous concerning—"

"Yes, I know." He looked up at his friend with apprehension and determination roaring through him. He'd have this moment of privacy. "Five, ten minutes at the most. Surely you see she's upset and I must help."

Sitting on the edge of the bench, the other man looked as if he wouldn't leave, but he did. With a small nod, he vacated and closed the door firmly behind him.

Time to truly calm her down and find out what had set her off the deep end into this crying fit. It was something he wasn't used to handling. The women around him were always ready for fucking and little else, especially not showing their emotional weaknesses.

"Shhh, we're all alone, now tell me what's the matter." Taking the stack of papers and purse from her, he put them on the floor by their feet. Then, holding her head cradled in one hand, he smoothed the other up and down her back and tried to resist moving farther down to her seriously wonderful ass. He knew the right decision had been made when Sui wrapped her arms around his neck and held him as close as he held her.

"Ish s ofg." The sound of her voice was followed by a healthy sniffle, but nothing she said made sense.

"Sorry, sweetness, I can't understand what you're saying."

She was talking jibberish but when she leaned back in his arms and Xer saw her beautiful blue eyes swimming in tears, surrounded by red and swollen lids, he felt his heart miss a beat.

"It as ofng," she said, moving to rebury her face in the crook of his neck.

"Settle down and say it all again. I can't help until I know what's wrong." He said this so gently and with meaning, she started crying all over again. "No, no, Sui, please don't cry." The edges of his nerves and patience were fraying.

Sitting up on his lap whilst sniffling, she rubbed the edge of her hand beneath her running nose and watched him with solemn eyes.

"It was no-nothing."

"I don't believe you, little one. Now again, what has reduced you to tears?" The smile on his face was there merely to put her at ease, he was ready to shake the answer from the beauty if she didn't spill it soon.

"It was stu-upid." She tried to dodge the question again.

"No, when I came upon you, you were genuinely upset. For the last time, why were you distressed and what turned the water works on?" He knew he was close to showing his impatience with her. Xer didn't like her denying him any part of her.

She drew a deep breath and whispered her answer.

"I didn't appreciate being called a Royal Mark. I'm a person, with a name and feelings. The minute he called me by that title, I felt what it must be like to be a Zandian woman, wanted for nothing more than sexual release. It was a demeaning, utterly degrading moment followed by the most chivalrous act a man of your standing could have made. You and your actions had me crying."

Before he could say a word and ask what he'd done, she rewrapped her arms around his neck, leaned over and kissed him. Lips laid against each other before she took the initiative and opened her mouth, urging his to part. He couldn't deny her seductive call, this was what he wanted as well.

It was difficult but he tried hard not to take control of their kiss. Xer enjoyed her coming to him for what she needed, be it emotional or physical. Using the fact her attention was focused elsewhere, he used both hands on her lovely hips and moved her around until she straddled his lap. The position called for her to lean forward, bringing her breasts up against his chest and he was ready to indulge himself.

The door was suddenly thrust open and Rol called out as they all started piling back inside. "My apologies, but the situation out here is quickly moving toward something we don't want to be in the middle of. It's time we left."

Both Sui and Xer looked out the vehicle's smoked glass and were surprised to see how they'd not stopped in a quiet neighborhood or even pulled off to the side of the road. Where they'd actually stopped was in the middle of a very popular shopping district, and the car was now the center of attention from a crowd. The driver had taken the demand to stop literally and they were in the middle of the road causing a disturbance, or so they guessed from the muffled sounds seeping inside.

The two looked at each other and couldn't hold back the laughter.

"Honestly, I heard nothing!" She gave her excuses, not bothering to try and hold back the loud gales escaping her lips.

"Neither did I, little one, neither did I." Trying to regain some sort of order, he looked over at his friend and was ready to lambaste him for not correcting the matter, then realized he hadn't given him an opportunity to do that.

"I apologize, Rol. The worry and inconvenience was unintended." It was unlike him to act this rashly, nor did he often have to offer apologies for his actions. However, this was his best friend. He'd acted improperly and put them all in danger. His only defense was that Sui'd needed his undivided attention and that took precedence.

Rol rolled his eyes, and before Xer could say anything further, the transport took off with a burst of energy, not the usual well-executed departure the driver would normally have made.

This sent everyone into fits of laughter.

Sui made to move off Xer's lap. Instead he stopped laughing and gripped her hips more firmly. "No, stay right where you are and kiss me again."

"Xer?" Leaning in, she whispered for his ears alone. "Please, could we continue what we were doing later? When we're alone, or at least under conditions feeling less like we're the night's entertainment?"

Maintaining his grasp, he shifted his head to speak softly into her ear. "As long as you stay where you are." After receiving her nod of acceptance, he placed a gentle kiss on her neck, right below her ear, near where her virus chip and infertility device had been placed. She still hadn' realized he knew the truth about her origins. In all matters pertaining to this woman, he'd be patient and wait for her to tell him.

Pressing her closer against his chest, he held her and continued to rub his hand in a soothing gesture up and down her back.

Over her head he caught the eye of Rol who faced him. There was a very serious expression on his friend's face, as if he was weighing a matter of great worth. After a moment, the man he trusted implicitly nodded, and Xer took it as an acceptance of how much he cared for this gentle woman and her being a part of his life.

೮ೈ೦೮

The date started most surreally, making Sui wish she'd never agreed to it in the first place.

Obviously it hadn't occurred to anyone how she may want to change from her work clothes for something more appropriate. For all the emotional upheaval and work, she felt completely worn out. They arrived at one of the most popular eating establishments in the city and the greeter seemed to have been expecting them.

They were ushered to a quiet, romantic table in a private corner, where Xer pulled the seat out for her and ensured she was comfortable before moving to take his. Shortly thereafter, a server arrived with a bottle and two glasses of a bubbly beverage, which tickled her nose. After settling the bottle in a cold stand, he turned and promised to return with a list of the food items available.

Looking around the top-rated dining facility, she noticed how, despite the place being very busy, there was a band of tables separating theirs from everyone else. The occupants of these tables were a mix of the prince's security and Zoolopean team members. The couplings of tough-looking men, all who appeared ready to take on anyone who tried to harm His Royal Heir Apprentice, was odd enough to draw a great deal of attention.

Actually it was pretty funny, watching all these huge, muscled men sitting at tables for two, and yet not looking remotely romantic.

"Have you ever been someplace without your security detail?" She had led a typical young woman's sheltered life up to the time she'd left Zandia so this was an interesting moment for her to observe, and she was curious to see how the lack of privacy affected him.

"I've never been on something like this—a date. I'm not entirely sure what we're supposed to do, but I do know I'm not supposed to kiss, touch or fuck you here. How about helping me out, what does an Earther normally do on these outings?"

"You've never dated at all?"

"No, it's, ummm, different back home."

"Okay, well, a date is basically used to get to know each other on a less superficial level in a neutral non-threatening place."

"Non-threatening? Am I scaring you again? Why, Sui? What have I done this time?"

"No, no you haven't done anything wrong. Remember, you asked me on a date. I only used the word to show how no one has an advantage of it being my place or yours, and, this is especially important for a woman. If the date is horrible, they can escape to their own space without having to try and evict the other person." She didn't think she was explaining herself well. He had a look on his face clearly stating he was confused and wasn't sure why he was here.

"Oh." Xer took another sip of the bubble drink, obviously mulling over what she'd said. "So a date is to get to know the other person outside of the sleeping area. Why? Don't people who date have sex?"

"Hmmm. Yes, but first they want to get to know each other better to see if there's something more between them."

"More of what?"

"Love is mainly what they're looking for. They date to see if they're compatible, care for the other person, maybe see a future together. There are many things dating accomplishes."

"Don't they know how they feel about another person at once?"

"You mean sexual attraction."

"No, no, I don't, Sui. When your voice reverberated through the arena, my cock went from just being there to hard and ready to come. Shit, every man in the stadium did, but we're not discussing that right now. It doesn't mean I wasn't aware of a certain intensity racing through my core. But when I saw you, it all leaped into the unimaginable...what?"

"Oh, well, um, nothing. You were saying?" She wasn't sure she wanted to know what he'd been about to say, but there was some part of her that really did.

"Yes! I may have marked you, Sui, but I fully intend to claim you." His attention was intently focused on her, sure of her acceptance of his decision.

"What?" Shocked, she couldn't believe what she'd just heard. To claim her meant going back to Zandia.

"Claim you, Sui Erom, as my path-mate for life." He looked surprised she wasn't throwing herself at him in joy over this new plan for their future. She imagined he thought every female dreamed of being swept up by their prince, but she didn't.

"No, you can't!" This wasn't happening to her, no matter how much she may have hoped for such a man, this official coupling would surely be the end of a chance for a free life.

"Why not?" Brows drawn together, he seemed genuinely puzzled and didn't look particularly happy over her lack of delight with his plan to claim her.

"Because!"

"Why, Sui? Explain it to me."

"I ca..." Before she could finish her declaration, out of the corner of her eye she noticed a member of the wait staff, a woman, was making her way through the band of tables. Sui didn't want to talk about something so important in front of a stranger. But the waitress took matters where none of them had expected.

"You don't want this pale thing, Your Royal Heir Apprentice, not when you can have..." The woman, who Sui thought was a Nazon, spoke loudly as she unbuttoned her top. Her actions made it appear as if she was going to strip for the prince. This just didn't fit what she knew about this all female society. It's common knowledge they don't like men in a sexual way.

Stunned, Sui couldn't believe this was happening, then she noticed the woman's odd movement as she reached across her stomach and under her arm. Not liking the motion, Sui quickly looked toward Rol for help and found him running, closing the distance between them, but he was too far away.

Although Rol was making his way toward them, she reached out and used all the physical power she possessed and pushed Xer and his chair backwards. The momentum took her with him—or maybe it was his arms reaching out to wrap around her waist—either way they both fell to a heap on the ground. She felt a sharp pain but dismissed it as an awkward landing.

"*No!*"

"You stupid freakish female!" The woman screamed her anger. Quickly, the crazy lady was surrounded by the Zandian security detail and restrained.

Meanwhile, Rol and the man who'd been her shadow all day boldly collected them from the floor and hustled the duo from the open and unsecured space of the restaurant.

Deafening screams and shouts had erupted from the other patrons and followed the group as they raced through the kitchens and out the back door. Very shortly after they stepped outside, their vehicle screeched to a halt before them. Sui found herself thrust into the back so fast she landed on the floor.

Shouts gradually slipped away as a heavy weight suddenly landed on top of her back and everything faded into blackness.

Chapter Thirteen

"Sui!"

"Sui!"

There were two different men calling her name, one deep voice sounded more panicked than the other, but neither was able to find solid footing as she spiraled in and out of consciousness. Her brain couldn't hold a clear thought. Everything was fuzzy, although she could feel both her hands were being held and rubbed.

"Sui!"

She wasn't being jostled around. Someone was gently holding her head completely still, and yet it hurt.

"Please, little one, open your eyes..."

There was a voice she knew, it said the most outrageous things in her dreams. If it didn't hurt so much, she'd open her eyes just to see his handsome face again.

"...I know it must hurt..."

Oh no, could he read her thoughts? Despite the pain, she knew such a skill being held by him couldn't be good, not for her.

"...but I need to know you're okay..."

What, had something happened to her? Was this why she hurt?

"Please, sweetness, show me those beautiful blue eyes." There was a sense of desperation for some reason she didn't like hearing from him, and at the same time it surrounded her with a warm glow.

She struggled to open her eyes and it took effort. Lids flickered and promptly closed again when pain burst across one orb. Her hand immediately made to move up, feel what was wrong or just cover and hold it until the pain slipped away. But whoever held the appendage wasn't releasing it, so she tried the other. It took a minute but eventually the person who held one of her hands moved it up to where she was injured.

Gently the hand led her finger along the edge of a slash running from her forehead down over her eyebrow ending a hairsbreadth before her eye. The slash may be painful, but it felt superficial. She'd heal.

Despite the discomfort, once again she slowly opened her lids and instantly found her gaze held by Xer's dark brown eyes exploding with emotions, and concern was the most obvious.

"There we go, now I see you're okay. Stop, Sui." His other hand landed over her stomach in a bid to hold her down. "Don't move. The medic should be soon," he whispered.

"What happened?" Her voice was quiet, she knew it was a mere whisper, but to her it sounded deafening.

"Shhh, we'll talk about it later, for now stay quiet." After he put her hand back to rest at her side, his finger returned to stroke softly down the side of her face, leaving her feeling cherished, protected, and loved.

His request sounded perfectly reasonable to her and she went to nod her agreement, only the small movement sent an explosion off in her head.

"Ohhh." The pain was almost unbearable. She looked up at her lover and found him frowning fiercely at the person who sat to her other side. Curious to see who held his displeasure, she closed her lids and reopened them, looking the other way.

Rol.

Before she could ask what the problem was between the two friends, there was a quick tap on a panel before it swung open. Neither man moved to leave her side.

In the dim light, an older man with a bald head and incredible level of physical fitness that labeled him Zandian to Sui, walked in to her line of sight. He held a medicinal wand, which clearly said he was the medic they'd been expecting.

After some shifting about, the man was at her side. He quickly and efficiently set about checking her various statistics. Using two fingers, he gently opened her wounded eye and flashed a pinpoint of light into the orb. Her headache was unbearable, made worse by the bright flash, but something niggled at her mind. She was sure there was something important she should remember about having a Zandian medicinal man this near her body.

Once the medic confirmed she wasn't injured in any other way, he stood up and spoke softly to the prince.

"My Royal Heir Apprentice, she'll be fine. A simple headache-away dosage should solve her most pressing difficulty." Keying something into the wand, he placed the tip to her neck and pressed a button, injecting the appropriate dosage.

"Clean the wound with a disinfecting swab, and a bit of HATP on her gash, all this should help heal and close the wound without scaring. I'll leave two doses of each, apply in the morning after she's, ummm, visited the wet room." He pulled a sealed packet from his coat pocket and tore it open, gently swiping the wad over the wound. Next he inputted a few sequences into the wand, set the tip to his finger and pressed the button. From the end oozed a clear gel, which he carefully spread over the wound.

"The bump and burst vessel in her eye will be fine in a few day's time. For the next few hours, keep the room lights down and quiet, but don't let her sleep for a full ten to twelve hours. Her head took a good bash and needs to find its equilibrium again. If she starts to feel ill, won't eat or loses her balance, contact me immediately, and we'll do the full scan."

When he stepped back from where she rested, Sui realized at no point had he addressed her, asked her how she was feeling, what hurt, nothing. To him, she was a female Zandian, merely a body, and it hurt enough to bring moisture to her eyes. It was a reminder of why she'd never be completely happy back on Zandia.

"Why are you crying?" Xer leaned down and spoke with her quietly. "Does your head still hurt?"

She shook her head, not wanting to sink back into the dark pit of anger again. The memory of someone setting out to possibly hurt him swamped her and she allowed the tears to slip down her cheek unchecked. He laid down beside her. Rol, who'd held her head, slowly moved away and Xer carefully replaced it with his arm, surrounding her with his presence.

"I was very scared for you," she confessed as she placed a gentle kiss on his lips.

"You remember what happened?"

"Bits and pieces. I remember a Nazon came up to our table and was fumbling with her clothes like she was going to strip and it didn't seem to be something they'd normally do. Next thing I remember, we're running through the kitchens and I'm landing on the floor of the vehicle. After that is nothing until I heard you telling me to wake up. What happened?"

Silence met her question. He was looking at her with something in his eyes, but it was too dark for her to see clearly. She wasn't sure what it was, but it was shouting something at her.

"It's been reported the woman has been following Xer's movements since his arrival in the American sector. Her plan was to try and pass as a Pelokian, seduce, then assassinate him, making her escape while everyone thought them still abed." Rol offered the explanation in a succinct and efficient manner. "Your presence changed everything and she came at you both with a knife, catching you in the face."

"But why? You've done nothing to harm anyone from Nazon." She looked at him with her heart in her eyes, there was no way she could hide her feelings when someone threatened his life.

"Thank you, little one, but you must know there will always be someone who doesn't like me or what I represent. Now, I beg of you to never put yourself in front of danger like that again. I don't ever want to experience another moment like the one we just had." He was very serious but he kissed her gently as if she were still an open wound.

They laid there together, sharing, touching—wait a minute!

"Ummm, Xer, where are my clothes?"

"When we arrived here, I took them off you, searching for wounds. We didn't know if all the blood was coming from your head or someplace else as well. We stripped and checked you over." It all sounded good but she still wasn't buying it.

"Liar, you wanted me naked as the day I was born." Sui called it as she saw it, even if she was still woozy.

After a long minute, he answered.

"Not completely bare, you still wear my mark." The large rough hand holding her hip, keeping her pressed against him, moved down and gave the chain coming from her ass a gentle tug.

Now that was something she clearly remembered. All day his mark had been tormenting her, leading her passions to rest on the edge, begging for a release, only to retreat in disappointment. With a multitude of emotions flooding her, she knew this cresting of her desire would be satisfied.

"Ohhh."

"I need you right now, Sui," Xer said as he rolled her to her back and made room for himself between her legs. "Tell me, are you in too much pain for this?" Cradling her head, he used his thumbs to smooth along the soft skin next to her eyes.

Shaking her head, she let him know how her need for him was just as necessary. Wrapping her legs up around his waist, her arms stretched up and out, and she told him of her need.

"Take me, I'm yours." The last words she spoke had been carefully chosen, because in her heart she belonged completely to him. Although she tried to keep it lighthearted. There'd been enough of the dire and serious with the assassination attempt.

Bracing himself on one elbow, he used his other hand to shift the fringe of his mark aside and lodged his cock inside the opening of her pussy. The crown of his rod wasn't nearly enough to offer her a chance at instant satisfaction, but she knew it would be coming her way sooner rather than later.

"You certainly are all mine." He watched her intently and slowly rocked in and out of the lush opening to her slit. With his hand still between their legs, he played with the strands of beads lining the chain of his mark. Collecting the excess allowed him to both tug on the line to unsettle the end buried in her backside and torment her trapped clit in the front.

"Ummm, delicious."

"Soon I'll present you with a larger onyx stone for you to wear in your ass. And soon I'll take you in this tight orifice and I most certainly don't want to hurt you." His wicked words played with her already tenuous hold on her passionate needs.

"Hmmm." Her attention scattered when he pinched her nub harder, giving another firm pull on the chain.

"You enjoy my mark, don't you? Something of me is always inside of you, teasing you, preparing you, helping your lustful nature to rise even further—continuously reminding you of us fucking."

"Oh Xer!"

In one thrust, he buried himself until his balls pressed against her ass. Using two fingers, he spread her lower folds, flicked her clit to make sure the bundle of nerves remained hard and exposed, then subtly changed his position so as he thrust, his groin scraped over the bundle of nerves.

"Yes! Oh yes!" Using her legs, she squeezed him closer.

He moved even more intently, in and out, without pausing. Their breath expelled in great gasping grunts and groans each time he thrust his full length into her clasping warmth. She moaned with a feeling of loss when he made the long pull out of her depths.

"No! No, come back, give me all of that big beautiful prick."

Her words were apparently all it took for him to ramp it up. She needed completion and Sui believed he needed to give it to her! Xer moved his arm, braced himself on both forearms, and started to thrust, over and over, inside her pussy. There was no chance for her to clench and hold him tightly. He was pounding in and out, not stopping.

"Fuck, sweet petite, you have the most delicious slit. Do you hear how wet you are, lots of luscious honey there to ease my way as I plow through your tight channel."

"Ungh!"

"Come apart for me, Sui. Let me feel you climax around my cock."

"Xer!" She loosened the grip she had on his hips.

"Come, come for me, baby!"

"Oh yes, yes, Xer!" She screamed as she splintered around his pistoning cock.

He looked down and watched as the orgasm took hold of her. Her slit tried to grasp hold of his rod, hold it firmly in place, and not allow him to easily retreat from her moist warmth.

"I love you." Leaning down, he laid a kiss on her mouth.

Gasp!

Chapter Fourteen

"Tell me what's in your heart, Sui, tell me now."

"Xer?"

"I see it in your eyes, feel it in your body," he moved a hand to hold her leg bent at the knee and pressed to the bed, "...especially here in your pussy." Xer started out slowly, sliding in and out of her damp clasp, pulling juice out coating his dick. "I hear it when we love..."

Slow and easy, it was maddening! Her immediate needs had been satiated and yet were once again uncontrollable. She wanted to feel his climax beating its own rhythm inside her.

"Xer?"

"I hear it in your voice..." He picked up speed, pounding in and out of her.

"Uhhh, please."

"Tell me, baby, tell me." He was incredibly big and hard.

"Yes! Yes, I love you, ahhhh! Xer!"

"Shit! Sui!" One thrust was all it took. He was fully imbedded in her and he let loose. She could swear he had seed coming from the bottom of his balls, because each load he shot felt like it had the velocity of a rocket behind it. He grunted with the intensity of his climax as it took over his body.

He collapsed atop her and she enjoyed having him there, even if he was a little heavy. When her breath came back, she tuned in to his kissing her shoulder and followed the line up her neck to her ear. He rubbed his nose along the way and she loved it, but something was still niggling at her mind, something wasn't right.

"I claim you, Sui, as my chosen path-mate. To always be at my side, be I prince, king or pleb."

With his dick still hard and pulsating in her pussy, he rose to his knees and, using her legs, pulled her even farther onto his hard-on.

"Wait!"

"No waiting, Sui."

He reached to the side and grabbed something he must have put on the bed earlier. Following his movement, she saw the room was full of people, a mix of the security staff and his speedball team members. She should've realized they were here but had been too involved with their loving, she'd even forgotten about Rol being there. They were all solemn, although in her quick glance at them she saw a few with their hands holding tight to their hard-ons. At least they were mostly dressed this time.

"Xer?"

"You are mine in all ways…"

He left the words hanging. She knew he was waiting for her to reply with the formal acceptance. There'd been no time to think about what she'd do if he claimed her. She hadn't thought it possible until he'd mentioned it earlier at the restaurant. Although, if she put her mind to it, she guessed Rol had warned her this morning. She looked to the other man and found him beside them on the bed, watching her with a gaze that said everything would be all right, to trust in her feelings.

Or had she hoped to see it and therefore put it there?

Sui looked back at Xer, took in everything about him, and the minutes passed by silently. He didn't rush her nor offer any pressure, but waited patiently for her to speak the traditional female Zandian response, although she thought the wait must be difficult for him. Honestly, there was only one thing she wanted, and it may break her to do it, but she loved him and would support him.

Taking a deep breath she gave him his words.

"...I am yours in every way."

Sui watched as he leaned down, bit her already hard nipple and placed a black onyx shield over the aureole, carefully closing the latch. Her mouth dropped open to see the hard tip poke through a hole. Fine chains dripped down from around the disk and each ended with bright aquamarine stones. He placed the twin onto her other nipple while she watched him, pinching the nipple and snapping the disk shut, and firmly closing the tiny clamp. The matching breast jewelry not only went well with his mark but they kept her nipples hard and poking straight out, ready for him to soothe, like her clit and ass.

Sui watched as he took in her body wearing only pieces he'd placed on her and, incredibly, she felt him grow harder inside her eager slit.

He moved her leg to match the other, leaving her spread wide open for him. She knew what was next, to consummate their pledge in the time honored tradition of his taking possession of her body. What was against tradition was the promise he gave to her as they made love.

"I don't want you to change one bit." He thrust his cock into her, hard, and his eyes glued to the tiny pelt covering her mound as he spoke. "Not one hair on your head or sweet pussy is to be removed." His thumb came over and started to strum her excited clit. "You'll wear my jewels each day, be ready for me as I am always ready for you." His gaze rose to rest on her large breasts with the hard pink tips poking through the hard black circular disks. "We are partners, never be afraid to disagree or offer me an opinion." Again, he pushed hard and she saw his eyes dilate further while he watched the jeweled ends snake around and snap against her breasts and their eager tips.

Raising his lust-filled eyes to meet hers, he moved his hands to rest beside her head and started to plunge hard and fast into her depths. "Love me, please don't ever leave me, just be mine."

With tears in her eyes, she gave him her acceptance. "Yes, yes, I'm yours, Xer, all yours. I'll stay at your side, always be ready for you—no matter what." Sui reached up and rubbed her hands over his smooth dome and whispered the last request between them. "All I ask is for you treat me with care and respect, and never as a handy sex object."

Suddenly he stopped moving and looked honestly surprised at her words. Sui knew they'd have to have a talk later about how they saw the future, because she was scared.

His Royal Heir Apprentice resumed fucking her and seemed to be struggling to hold his climax, while she had no desire to hold off the inevitable and came with a lusty scream.

"Xer!"

"My woman!"

"Yes, mine." Sui whispered after he collapsed on her, her slit still pulsing wildly around his throbbing cock, holding it deep inside her heated depths.

This, whatever it was between them, would work. They'd make it work together.

Part III:
Bound and Enthroned

Chapter Fifteen

"Woman, enough of this secrecy! I swear on all you hold dear if you don't explain to me right this minute why you pretended not to be Zandian, I'll—grrrr! Answer me right now! Why do you deny being from Zandia?"

"Don't get all testosterone-amped with me, Xer Rieh!"

"Sui!"

"Okay, but give me a minute! Stop pacing around, you're making me nervous."

"Oh please, you jumped in front of an assassin's blade, nothing can make you uneasy."

There was a heavy pause before she quietly answered him, not looking to see how her words affected him.

"You do."

Those two words instantly stopped his tirade. He sat on the side of the sleep platform, looked at her, and waited. It took her a moment because she couldn't remember seeing him this focused on one thing at the same time as being completely still and patient.

It'd been almost a full week since he'd claimed her and obviously he couldn't wait any longer for her to spill everything. They hadn't left his official quarters in the Zandian Embassy, specifically their sleeping area. But this morning, Sui stated she was well enough to go back to work while he preferred to keep her safe, protected, and at his side. Her need to get back to a normal routine brought the issue of her original dishonesty back to the forefront between them.

The end of her deception was finally here and deep down she knew it was for the best, but it was going to be a tough road to follow. Sui needed strength and all her wits about her in order to state her case clearly and concisely. There were many things she needed to accomplish through this one confession, although she couldn't allow the importance to weigh her down. When all was said and done, she hoped he'd see how wrong life on Zandia was for her in particular and all women in general, and maybe their future could be better.

Despite the large scope of her problem, it was very important to her that this man before her see and understand why she took the risks she'd taken to live a fulfilling life. It mattered because he was her heart.

"Yes, you've been right all along. I was born on Zandia, part of the Seccus fold. Ambassador Ero Seccus is my father. My pathline was determined to be emotive, and right before I was to finish at the National Education Institute, my fold leader was called away and I decided to hide out on his transporter. Earth was where he was sent and I've remained here ever since."

Sui realized, despite expecting her confession, she'd still managed to surprise him with a very brief outline of how her life on Earth had come to be.

"Why did you—ah shit, Sui, you could've been killed. Wait, your fold leader knows!"

"Please, let me finish." She sat beside Xer and turned toward him, grasping hold of both his hands in hers. The tension riding throughout his body was almost palatable, but she held on and waited for his eyes to refocus on her. "I promise to answer any questions you have, but first let me get everything said."

Taking another breath, she brought one of his hands up to her cheek and leaned into it. She closed her eyes to find her center and take all the strength and comfort she could from having him at her side. With her eyes closed, she continued in more detail.

"The emotive path was never a suitable one for me. I love my fold, my entire clan, and will always feel a need to offer them support with all my being, but deep inside me there was a voice calling for much more. Like traditional pathlines, I wanted to experience the love of a man, physically. I needed to feel necessary and wanted, to be everything for my lover—to be a partner.

"Throughout my childhood and my formal educational years, I saw how men were allowed to treat women and none of it appealed to my sense of equality. Yes, I see us all as equals. I know, I know, there are obvious differences between men and women. But to me, and in my soul, I see the sexes as being both mentally and physically equal. And, Xer, the female's role in Zandian society is very wrong. They—no, we—are much more than a body to offer sexual release.

"Here on Earth, I'm a productive member of society. I support myself and am happy at the end of each day knowing I participated to the best of my ability."

The frown on his face deepened and his mouth opened as if ready to speak had her rushing to complete her thoughts.

"No, please, let me finish. This planet, this sector in particular, has offered me many opportunities at having a life full with purpose and challenges, and yes, it makes me happy. I did look for a man to share—wait!" She pressed a finger against his lips, hoping to hold back the tide of words threatening to escape. She was almost finished. "A man to share my life with, but none fit. Then you came into my world and quickly became much more than Prince Xer III, my Royal Heir Apprentice to the Zandian throne—you are the man I love and want to build a life with."

Sui took her finger away and steeled herself for the barrage guaranteed to come.

"You could've been hurt, even killed, and no one would ever have known!" The words burst forth with anger behind them but she knew it was mainly concern.

"Yes, but it was well worth any risk to feel like a necessary human being. To have a chance at a fulfilling life."

While his voice was raised, she tried to remain calm, although it was becoming more difficult as he appeared very upset. She'd remain strong and not weaken in her position. This discussion was too important not to hold firm to her beliefs.

"Don't try to find reason or logic with any of this. Here, let me hold you for a moment." He pulled her close and held on, tightly.

With one act from him, she felt everything would be all right. They'd find a way to work through this rough patch.

"You will never, ever, leave me. Swear an honesty oath to me on this, Sui!" He held her head so they were nose to nose. No longer was the moment gentle and loving, it'd swiftly moved into something she didn't like.

"This relationship of ours is a partnership, not a dictatorship, Xer, nor will it ever be."

"Sui, give me your honesty oath now or you'll never leave my side again."

"Don't do this to me. Did you hear anything I've just told you?"

"I heard how you've been living by yourself on an alien planet, without any resources to ensure your safety. Now give—me—your—honesty—oath!"

While she remained seated on the side of the sleep platform, he stood up before her, hands on his hips, looking completely unyielding and totally aggressive. Looking down at her folded hands resting uselessly in her lap, she thought about how she'd gambled and appeared to have lost. She didn't see any way out of this. Not ready to give up so easily, she sat there and racked her brain, looking for a loophole to be used for her benefit later. But in the thick air surrounding the couple, she came to terms with her fate. The fight wasn't over yet, but she'd continue until the battle was won. This man before her was her heart. There was no denying it and compromise was called for here.

"I promise to never leave your side without your permission."

He nodded and continued to stand there, his eyes darting around her face and the curls resting around it. There was fire in his browner than brown eyes, she could feel the heat singeing her hair.

For many minutes each remained where they were, neither offering an opening to the other nor softening their stance.

The tension was almost unbearable but she wasn't sure she had the energy to break it, not when she felt so broken. Xer moved quickly, and Sui wasn't ready for it. Not that she would've done anything to fight him as he pulled her into his arms again, although it surprised her enough to raise her damp gaze up to his.

"Your safety means everything to me, and makes it important enough for an honesty oath. It doesn't automatically follow that your life is over, or that I'll treat you as if you were a lesser being—you should have more faith in me, Sui. It hurts when you don't."

"I'm sorry, it wasn't my intention not to have belief in you. I'm used to taking care of myself. You must know I love you, but there's much I don't know about you."

"Well, here I am, ask me."

The sincerity and openness radiating from him surprised her. He was right, why didn't she come out and tell him of her concerns?

"Okay. Do you see anything wrong with how women are treated on Zandia?"

"Yes." There was no hesitation or pause in the powerful man's response. "There are no excuses for this, nor is it any single entity's fault. We come from an established society choosing to remain static in many ways and not learn from others as we're exposed to them. As a culture, we close ourselves off from outside influences. We say it's because we are located far away from everyone else, but I think those with all the power see no reason for change. And then there are people who will always see it as easier to stay the same. One of my missions is for Zandia to no longer be the butt of the Universe's jokes when it comes to our way of life."

Xer spoke with such passion and energy, she felt he was ready to do something and not wait for it to be done.

"Oh." It was shameful for her to admit how he'd surprised her.

"Don't be upset, little one." He moved until he sat on the edge of the bed with her in his lap.

"But you're right, I had no faith in you." Sui reached up and wrapped her arms around his neck and held him close, leaving her nose pressed against his neck. This quiet moment, in his arms, smelling his special scent, was precious and she'd always remember it as giving her a sense of acceptance and, yes, most assuredly love.

"You're being too hard on yourself. I understand it'll take time for you to trust me. I suggest we use what we have here, an opportunity to be relatively alone, and get to know each other better. Especially our hopes and dreams for the future, both for ourselves and yes, for Zandia, because our bond will surely be tested in the future." One hand held her close while the other soothed by rubbing up and down her back.

"Hmmm, it's a daunting thought." She wondered how she'd made it this far without it coming into her mind. "What if your parents don't approve of me as your claimed path-mate and deny us a right to be officially joined? What if they hold against us both all I've done, or—"

"Shhh, everything will be fine." Xer laid his lips across the top of her head. "Remember, you're not alone in this, you have me. We can do anything together."

Lifting her head, she looked into his beautiful brown eyes shining with confidence. Unable to help herself she leaned forward and laid her lips against his, absorbing the texture and flavor of his mouth. Sui tilted her head to the side as she used the tip of her tongue to run along the dark seam, coaxing him to open up so she could taste him further.

"Hmmm, you are a very addictive man, my Royal Heir Apprentice," she whispered while nibbling on his upper lip, pulling it gently with her front teeth.

"As are you, my love. Now come back here and ride me while I play with your new onyx plug." He moved them back on the platform until his head rested against a cushioned headboard. After she was settled, straddling his lap, she slid over the fierce hard-on he sported.

Slowly she started to sink down over his solid length, savoring the feeling of how complete his possession of her body truly was even at times like this when she controlled their fucking. The new, larger cylinder buried in her back rose took getting used to. It would take time to acquaint herself with its presence. The original piece had reminded her of the passion he'd promised her. The larger stone filling her back passage, and the bejeweled onyx shields she now wore around her nipples, clearly stated it was guaranteed he'd follow through as long as she remained ready.

Not to worry, her revenge would come when he least expected it.

With Rol's help, a wide onyx ring with raw aquamarine rocks dangling from various length of chains had been created for him and would match his mark and claiming pieces she wore. The ring was for him to wear on his cock, ensuring he was always hard and ready to please his mate.

Sui fell forward, bracing her weight with hands resting on his chest. Xer was using one hand to tease the smooth stone in and out of her ass, driving groans of need from her deepest depths. He twisted the piece while moving it back and forth, reminding her of its solid presence, all while she moved her dripping pussy on and off his solid dick.

"You're very sexy, baby girl." Xer growled as she worked her wicked way with his body.

"Ohhh!"

She felt his other hand resting on the curve of her hip, not helping but resting there, letting her find the rhythm that spoke to her and it was hard and fast.

"Fuck me, there you go, take what you need from me."

"Ohhh, Xer." She gasped, already breathless.

"Come on, baby, I can feel your pussy squeezing me hard." He teased her mind as much as her body with his words.

"Yes! Ohhh!"

"I see your nipples are...shit!"

She knew the bright red tips were poking through the centers of their shields. The faster and harder she moved, the more the beads whipped against her breasts, working them up more and more.

"Ahhh!" Sui's climax suddenly hit her, holding his cock captive in her tight silken depths, squeezing him hard only to have the muscles relax and tighten, again and again.

"Ungh!" Her tight, pulsating clasp beat around him, pulling jets of seed from him. They burst forth, splashing against the walls of her pussy.

"Shit, baby, you're going to be the death of me!" He wrapped his arms around her back and enfolded her body as she collapsed over him in exhaustion.

"Love you so much," she whispered against his neck.

"Don't worry anymore, you're my everything." Large capable hands smoothed over her nude back. "Together we can handle anything."

"I don't know if I can be comfortable with so much responsibility, especially over other people," she confided.

"We have plenty of time to work through this, just remember you're not alone." Assurance and a note of acceptance laced his words.

He was right, there was plenty of time to worry about everything else.

Chapter Sixteen

After their passion had once again been spent, his cock still buried in her depths and his seed seeping out of her slit, they spoke quietly to each other. Eventually there were conditions they'd mutually agreed upon for Xer to be comfortable in her walking out the door without him at her side.

The most difficult and largest stumbling block for him had been an assurance of her safety. Once they'd settled on her having a security team following her everywhere, and he meant absolutely everywhere, then he'd been more willing to work on other items as well.

So much had happened, and despite this Sui was now back in her booth, preparing to call the last Zandian Zoolopean game in the competition. She'd had no doubt they'd make it to the finals, but she was surprised she hadn't killed their beloved captain before they got here.

There were two men standing outside the booth and another inside with her, all weighted down by their full suits of armor. Nobody could miss the fact of how well-protected she was, which drew a variety of reactions.

In the beginning, the reason she'd accepted Xer's conditions was to be able to continue working and go back to being a normal, yet productive, person. Unfortunately her workmates had found her new status as the claimed mate to a

Royal Apprentice too much to handle and complained how her guards created a tense work environment and left no room for them to get anything done. With regret, Sui had resigned sooner than she'd expected; however, it'd been an easier decision to make than she'd anticipated. She happened to love and was path-mated with an important man, one with enemies who wanted him dead or harmed. Now it was personal. They were her problem because she didn't want to see him hurt in any way.

None of this made him a saint. In fact, it didn't even make him minutely less frustrating. Because of his stubbornness, she'd missed calling a match. She wouldn't dwell on it, she was happy to be back. Sui continued her check and through her sound unit connected with the other translators there in the arena to participate in the final event. It was an honor for the Zoolopeans to be here and a tribute to their excellence. Unfortunately, for her it was also going to be her last job and she wanted to savor every moment.

As expected, the Zandians were the favorites but the challengers, the Jidian Jilocks, had definitely earned their right to be here. They were big, physical men. They lacked the athleticism and dexterity the Zoolopeans excelled in but nobody knew what the final outcome would be because heart, ego and pride were all elements not easily discounted.

In a quiet moment, she took the time to flick through her research on the Jilocks again and tried to familiarize herself with the proper pronunciation of their names. There had been some major, well-publicized mistakes made during this tournament and she didn't want to be one of those.

It had taken some time to find her comfort zone with the changes in her life but she finally felt centered and comfortable with her new place in the world. Image, and how Zandians and the Universe saw her, mattered. She didn't want to embarrass or become a liability to Xer.

The guard in the booth with her stepped up and lightly placed his hand on her wrist. She looked up and saw how he held his other hand pressed against his sound plug as he spoke quietly into the mic.

"Yes, sir." He took off his plug and held it out for her to take. "It's His Royal Heir Apprentice for you, ma'am."

Sui held up the plug to her other ear and pressed the mic.

"Hello, Xer?"

"Hello, gorgeous. I had to hear your voice before everyone else."

"Oh really, still having a little problem with, ummm, those trigger reactions?" She whispered the last words, quietly enough for her guard not to hear, but she was sure he had by the laughter he tried to hide behind an exaggerated cough.

"Big problem, my sweet petite."

She gave her guard a look and spun around in her chair.

"It certainly is and the fine piece of flesh is all mine, no matter who sees it in that revealing uniform you wear."

"Yours and only yours. Tonight I'll make you come more times than you can count. I'll ride you through your first orgasm to the next and keep fucking until you beg me to stop, and only then will I finally fill you up with all my seed."

"My, you certainly know how to seduce a woman."

"Not any woman, but my woman."

A tone in her plug sounded, reminding her there were ten minutes before she was officially to begin her duties.

"I must go, the first bell has sounded. Good luck."

"Enjoy yourself up there, and remember, my beloved sex goddess, I'm listening to you."

"Stop, I'm blushing!"

"Excellent."

"Bye."

"Bye."

She heaved a deep, love-sick sigh, turned back to the guard and handed him back his sound unit with her thanks.

"My pleasure, ma'am," the man said before he returned to his original position, prepared to protect her from any intruders.

Refocusing on the conversation taking place across the translators' private line, she heard a frantic discussion taking place and quickly realized she'd missed her check-in appointment.

"No, no, I'm here! I apologize, was called away on an impor—" She was cutoff and held her silence as a barrage of anger from her supervisor on this translation job was thrown at her. "No sir, I most certainly do not think I'm too important to do the job. I'm honored to handle the duties in the name of Zandia."

Briefly she was unsettled by the vehemence thrown down the line at her personally, but took it because she'd acted unprofessionally. Talking to her man on the company's time, no matter who he was, was wrong.

With hands shaking, she jumped right back into the mix and noted down the translator order and continued with the preparation for the fun but fast-paced manner in which the next couple of hours would move.

Another bell sounded. She listened to what was coming across her sound unit and moved her finger to touch her mic.

"All go from the Zandian desk. Countdown to the match start. Three—two—one—mark." She listened, pressed a few buttons as needed and finished the checklist. When the host's announcer began to speak to the arena crowd and locker rooms, Sui took a sip of water and closed her eyes for a moment, privately wishing her man the best game he ever had, and was ready.

"Good evening. Welcome to the Thirty-fourth Annual Universe Speedball Cup championship match between the Jidian Jilocks and the Zandian Zoolopeans."

Although she couldn't hear it in her soundproof booth, she smiled, sure a roar of excitement boomed around the enclosed stadium. There were a couple of monitors for her to watch the action, and at this moment, it was all about the fans and they looked like they were going wild.

The teams were introduced, and when it was time to introduce her man, Sui tried hard to keep it from being personal. The struggle abruptly ended when on the monitor she watched him stride out of the tunnel opening, stand with power and strength circling him, and looked up to her booth. This time he knew who owned the voice and had not only marked her, but claimed her as his path-mate. She sighed, it was obvious how at this moment, he was absolutely sure of his place in the Universe.

Her heart pounded and Sui crossed her legs to ease the ache rapidly building between them. She'd been here before and knew it would be a long couple of hours full of her needing this man before satisfaction would be hers.

The metal sphere dropped from the ceiling and play began.

From the beginning of the championship, it was believed by most fans that the cup was the Zoolopeans' to loose. The action was non-stop from the drop of the first sphere. Rol made the first hole, and the fans went wild. He was now the overall high scorer through the competition, the co-captain was very skilled, and never failed to bring in the points. By the end of the first period, they were two points up, but the Jilocks were fighting to stay within striking distance.

At the end of the third period, the Zoolopeans were only ahead by one point and Sui thought the play had moved beyond physical and into brutal. Elbows were being tossed about freely—one of the Zandian players ended up with his cheekbone shattered. As they came out onto the court for the final period, the team wore clear, protective, full-face masks. They were going for the win, and taking no prisoners along the way.

Xer won the drop and used his size and strength to intimidate the opposition as he ran down the center of the court, showing no mercy for anybody who made a move to stop him. Using his natural athleticism and skill, he seamlessly moved from the center over to the side and up the wall at the curved corner, all with enough momentum to allow him to lodge a sphere securely in the hole.

Sui jumped up with excitement at her man's masterful score, only he landed hard on his shoulder and wasn't moving by the time it came to her turn to make the scoring call. She was very worried. He didn't bounce right back like normal, more like rolled until he was up on his knees and looked over at Rol with a fierce expression before he struggled to his feet.

The crowd gasped in unison once they saw how his arm was hanging down at an odd angle. An injury time was granted and the team medic ran out onto the court floor. Although the team surrounded them, everyone watched as his body was manhandled. Xer let out a loud roar, which she heard through the medic's mic. As the men started to disperse, she saw his arm was back in place and he prepared to continue the game.

After finishing her call of the score, and without loosing a beat, she closed her translator mic and looked over at her guard. "Check on his condition now. Please." She had a very small window before she had to turn her sound unit back on. She noted for the audience how the Zoolopean captain was fine, and the game would continue. Meanwhile she was a mess.

There was limited space in the booth, but she took it all up and paced, keeping her eyes on the monitors and continuing to do her job as translator for the game but there was no joy in it, not until her bodyguard stepped up behind her and brought her to a standstill with his hand on her shoulder.

He leaned down and whispered softly into her free ear, "Separated shoulder, and truly is fine."

Nodding her head in understanding, she heaved a sigh of relief and continued on. She knew he must be in pain and didn't like being this far from his side. In a few minutes, the match was over and the Zandian Zoolopeans were once again named the Universe Speedball Champions.

The award service took place immediately following the match and was full of respectful sportsmanlike conduct—over the top grandiose statements of superior skill would be saved for later. During a photo-op between both captains and co-captains, an invitation was forwarded to the Jilocks team to come and play a series of matches on Zandia, with a similar offer returned in kind.

All while this was taking place, Sui was still doing her job, translating the award presentation and official interviews. Everything flowed well until Xer officially retired from the national speedball team. His announcement hadn't been a surprise to her, they'd talked about it together, but to hear him state it officially added one more link in the chain between them.

It also managed to open the floodgate for the voracious media hounds to venture forth and ask much more personal questions of Xer. Was it because of the assassination attempt? His claiming a path-mate? Has there been news of the king removing the crown and sword in order for his heir to ascend the throne?

This was the most awkward moment of her career. Being personally involved in the interview and yet at the same time having to remain detached enough to work the translation professionally.

A blush stained her cheeks and she was happy to be hidden in the booth anonymously situated above the court. Once the activity moved into the locker rooms, she continued working, but with more focus. She not only had no visual to rely on but there were a multitude of voices coming at her over the audio unit.

From the end of the match, it was a good hour until she finished her official duties and started working on completing her paperwork before heading below to sign out of the arena one final time. After she signed off her mic, removed the sound plug for the last time, she felt a twinge of sadness. Sitting back down in her chair, she looked at the board and fully took in the significance of the occasion.

Her independence was officially over.

Lost in her thoughts Sui was surprised when Xer picked her up, sat in her chair and moved her onto his lap, holding her close. Yes, this was a good reason for making such a major change.

Quickly and with conscious thought, she shook off the veil of solemnity she'd allowed to fall upon her. This wasn't a time to feel sorry for herself. This day could never be repeated and should therefore be one she looked back upon with great joy as she told their babies about the time she'd worked on the planet Earth and called the Zandians matches in the Thirty-fourth Annual Universe Speedball Cup.

"How is your shoulder?" Whispering softly, she slid a finger softly over the injured flesh.

"It's fine."

"No, really, it was difficult to see. I felt trapped, having to continue working but still being worried about you."

"Aren't you sweet."

"No, it isn't sweet, what it is, is upsetting."

For a long minute, he said nothing. "Now you know how I feel when you go out on your own."

Put in simple terms like that, she did understand. He hadn't been cruel and pulling her backwards like she thought, her lover had only been concerned for her welfare. She laid a soft kiss on his cheek and focused on entering her new life with as much energy and excitement as she had the one she was leaving. Sliding from her lover's lap, Sui settled herself between his knees.

"Ready for the festivities to begin, my gorgeous claimed mate?" She reached up and untied his loose trousers. There was nothing better than seeing how his cock was always eager to play. Joy bloomed through her as his rod popped right out, excited for whatever attention was coming its way.

"Yes, baby girl, we certainly are." As he answered her query, she couldn't take her gaze away from how his hand moved down and started to stroke his hard cock.

"You possess a beautiful cock, may I taste?"

"Of course, all you want."

Placing her hands on his smooth, strong thighs, she leaned down and teased the weeping tip with her tongue. She collected and savored a drop of cum decorating the tip, then took more as she was unable to stop from sliding her mouth down the hard length.

She felt his hands tunnel into her hair and hold her head as she moved on and off his length. Humming, she moved her mouth over his hard-on, enjoying every bit of his satin-covered steel, every hard ridge and smooth plane.

Sui moved her thumbs and teased his already firm balls, both felt ready to release their load. His displeased growl when she backed off brought a huge smile to her face. Oh, he was in for a wonderful surprise.

"I have a present for you."

"Now?"

"Oh, yes, this is the perfect time." She leaned over and dug through her bag until she found the sedately wrapped box. Pulling it out, she handed it to him and watched as he took off the paper. Eager to see what he thought of her answer to the jewelry he'd placed on her, Sui sat up and put her hands on his knees.

Xer lifted an eyebrow at her and took the cock ring out of the box, holding it up. Her bodyguard drew in a loud gulp of air. She turned to look at him before turning back to her mate, now worried she might have done something wrong.

"Well? What do you think?"

"Are you sure you want me to wear this?"

"I think it'd look handsome on you."

"You must be prepared to take the consequences."

"What do you mean?"

"This band will have me constantly hard, horny for relief. I'll be forever hounding you, wanting to fuck you at every moment."

"How would it be different from what you do now?"

He laughed and pulled her close, kissing her smiling lips. "Here, put it on me. Are you ready to take me in your beautiful ass, my sassy mate?"

Moving her mouth over his hard length again, moistening it to help ease the onyx ring with its dangling aquamarine rocks down until it rested right in front of his balls and flush against his groin. It truly was a wonderful piece, suited him with all its hard edges and solid appearance. She would love to see him walking around, completely nude, with these jewels around his cock. It'd be an incredible sight to bring her lusts to new heights.

There was no doubt in her mind she was ready for him to take her back passage.

"Oh yes, I'm definitely ready."

"Okay, but you tell me at any point if I'm hurting you, deal?"

"Deal."

After she stripped off her clothes, Sui turned and went down to her forearms and knees, shaking her tush to spur him on. The move sent her own jewels slapping against her body, driving her arousal even higher.

"Hurry up."

"No." He moved in behind her, spreading her legs even wider, and started to play with the onyx bullet she wore.

A cool liquid dripped along her crease, bringing her head around to look over her shoulder.

"What was that?"

"Something to allow my cock to slide through your ass as easily as it does your lubricious pussy."

Sui caught the eye of her bodyguard before all her thoughts scattered when Xer placed the head of his cock at her rear entrance. She wasn't sure why she looked between her legs, but she did, and there she saw the onyx bullet resting on the floor, although the hook remained firmly attached to her nub. It looked much smaller than his rod.

"Now relax, breath in, nice and easy. Wonderful, baby girl. There, the crown is in. Keep breathing, there you go, and again. Yes, there we are, a little more inside your ass." He moved the small bit he put in the back passage, slowly, in and out, adding a bit more of the liquid as he went. "Now on the next exhale, push out...yes, oh yes, perfect! Do you feel me sliding in? I'm almost there, keep pushing, yes, yes!"

She felt his cock, fully buried inside her ass, his balls rested heavily against her. Both his hands settled on her hips and he held her still as he slowly moved a small portion of his length out, then back in again.

"Sui?"

"Yes, yes, oh yes, give me more."

"Oh love, the pressure of the ring is so tight, I don't want..."

"Fuck me, Xer, please, take me now before I die."

As if her words were spoken directly to his rod, the jeweled hard-on pulsed in her channel, bringing a groan from her lips.

"Now, Xer, now!"

Slowly, he pulled most of his length out before slipping back down the tight channel. Gathering momentum, he moved a little faster until the ring pressed against her soft white rump. She felt him squeezing her cheeks, pulling them apart, then pressing them back together. Finally, he fucked her in earnest, in and out, ending with his balls and the rocks of aquamarine slapping her clit.

Spreading her legs wider, she was quickly on the edge of the wall, teetering, and with one more steady stroke in, out, and in again, she was sent falling over. As she came, Sui was surprised to notice how her back channel pulsed around Xer's plunging rod along with her empty slit, bringing him with her.

"Shit!"

He collapsed atop her and used a hand to hold her mound, pressing her tightly to him as he rolled them to their sides.

"Wow! The anal part was great, but the ring felt delicious!"

Xer tried to laugh but had no breath. "I can already tell neither of us will get anything done, we'll be going at it all the time."

"And the problem is?"

He pulled her closer, burying a couple of fingers in her wet pussy and nudged his still hard cock further in her back passage, causing her to moan with the lust he stirred.

"No problem, baby girl, no problem at all."

Chapter Seventeen

After they'd won the championship, there seemed to be no end to the celebrations.

Xer smiled fondly as his mind strayed back a few days to the stink and press of the locker room up to the sound booth and Sui. He'd known she'd have a difficult time leaving behind the last vestige of her independence and as soon as he could, he went up to be at her side for support. When he'd opened the door, he saw he'd been right, but as usual she'd turned him inside out.

He closed his eyes and rubbed a hand down between his legs, felt his rod harden at the memory and smiled. No matter how far she'd traveled from home, his path-mate would always be a Zandian in her sexuality. She thrived when expressing herself physically and excelled at pushing him beyond his breaking point. He also had no problem admitting she'd been right, she definitely wasn't suited for the emotive pathline she'd been directed to follow.

There was nothing he'd change about his love, she was perfect. He also understood this didn't mean they wouldn't have problems when back on Zandia.

During the media's attentions after the final he'd taken the opportunity to resign from the national team as a player. In the end, it hadn't been as difficult a decision as he would've thought. He'd always appreciate what the sport had given him, and would ensure the sport continued to thrive on Zandia, but it was time for him to move forward and take responsibility for his future, and for his planet.

What he hadn't expected was how his announcement had brought forth a frenzy of questions regarding his personal life. He'd stated a need to shift his focus as the reason, but the media had wanted something juicier and went looking for it. Of course he'd expected them to look at Sui, and had been conscious of how all the queries would be affecting her up in the booth while she worked. There'd also been no doubt in his mind she'd be having a difficult time maintaining objectivity and not allowing any personal emotions to enter her translations. But, as anticipated, she'd managed admirably.

Much of what they'd asked about had been a rehash from the assassination attempt, and from there everything had swiftly jumped over to Sui. He appreciated how there were people in the Universe who felt it was their right to know everything about his personal life. He didn't always like it but he understood people felt those in power owed their lives to the people. Knowing about human nature didn't necessarily make it any easier to handle the intrusion, especially now that he was mated. Xer wanted to keep her to himself, hold her close, and not share any part of her. Unfortunately he knew the personal invasion would never end and would only become progressively more difficult to handle if they let it get to them.

The demands on him as a Royal Heir Apprentice were immense, and now that there was a mate, they'd grown immeasurably.

Xer sighed heavily as his attention turned. In the aftermath of the assassination attempt made against him, and once it had become apparent his marked lover was going to survive, his only thought had been to delve instantly into the act of officially claiming her as his path-mate. He hadn't wanted another moment to go by where their future wasn't completely settled and clear to all.

That night was still a dark memory for him. As soon as they'd made it back to the Embassy after the attempt, the demand, both personally and officially, he return to Zandia had been waiting for him. But no longer was his concern for his parents. Now it was for a blonde beauty with incredible breasts. He'd needed to give his mate time to come to terms with the major change her life had taken. At the same time, he'd wanted to take the opportunity for them to become a solid couple, one who looked to each other first, all before returning home.

Selfish, maybe, but possessing this type of closeness would be an asset for them both once they were back home. Now it was time for them to take the next step together. He stood and walked over to the side of their bed and looked down at his mate. She was curled up on her side with her folded hands beneath her cheek, like a small child. It was time to leave this planet and he could honestly say it was the best trip he'd ever made. Xer moved a large finger through her silky curls. Who would have thought hair could be so seductive. Her sultry voice dancing around the arena may have drawn his attention, but physically her hair held him utterly captivated. He could picture her no other way.

With a smile, he pulled the sheet away from her body and snuggled up to her curved body. He sensed his mate was about to set a fire across Zandia. Many, many years ago, it had been determined by the medics board hair was full of diseases and should be stripped from the Zandian genome. The solution offered had been a drastic measure, one which the then ruler hadn't been willing to take, but an agreement had been made to a chemical, which discouraged hair growth, being added to the water supply.

Nudging his nose against the side of her neck, he enjoyed her tickling curls and decided her unintentional teasing would have to end, immediately.

"Wake up, my sweet petite."

She moaned and he pressed his hard-on further into her rear crease, nudging his mark.

"Today is the day we go home."

"Humph."

"Have you packed up everything you want to take back with you?"

All he got back in response to his question was another grumble.

"Is there anything you want to do before we board the transporter?"

Instead of an answer, she slid her sleepy gaze over her shoulder and met his, and he was lost. "I'd like to get more black mort to take back, and maybe one of those pretty glass apples as a memento."

"We certainly can. Are you okay making this trip back to Zandia?"

"Of course, although I'm not sure what I'll do to keep myself busy this time."

"Hello, what, do you think we can only fuck while on Earth?"

"Besides that! I don't want to wear you out before we even get there."

"Please, it isn't possible."

"Pshaw!"

She rolled over and Xer couldn't help himself from pressing a kiss on her soft lips. Sui snuggled closer. He lifted her leg over his hip and nudged the crown of his cock into her heated pussy. He was ready to show her all engines were set on go.

"Maybe we could talk about what my role will be as your joined path-mate."

Only Sui had the ability to give him pause in his quest for a climax.

"Yes, we can do anything and more. We can also discuss what projects you may want to take on."

"That would be wonderful." As she leaned in and kissed him deeply, all thoughts of how they'd occupy themselves on the long trip were forgotten.

Five hours later, they stepped onto the shuttle, which took them on a short journey to the local secured space waystation. He escorted his mate through the station, noting odd looks thrown at them as they made their way along various platforms toward his official transporter. Xer was reminded of exactly how difficult the situation Sui was about to face was actually going to be. He was expecting there to be challenges, and was sure she did as well, but they'd handle them together.

There was no second guessing how he'd turned her life upside down and he had no regrets either. They were meant for each other, all the upheaval would be worthwhile. Since the party where he'd marked her, they'd spent most of their time in the company of either team members or his personal security entourage, and all had been accepting of her. Of course he'd been aware of the rumblings about her unique appearance but it gave him no pause. He was sure the Zandian people would accept her as their future queen because of her intelligence and kindheartedness. Neither her need for independence, nor her unique appearance would be an issue.

It was well known how Zandians, whether consciously or not, preferred to be in groups, they weren't a solitary people.

Due to the very nature of her presence on Earth, her need for secrecy, and the obvious physical differences with others, Sui'd been forced into a secluded life, which went against her upbringing. While he was proud of her accomplishments, he still felt a great deal of fear of what could have happened and, as before, anger directed at her father came rushing forward. The man had much to answer for.

With his arm wrapped around her shoulder, he pulled her closer to his side and dropped a kiss onto her blonde curls as they walked down the hallway leading to the official transporters entry, going slowly in order to give her time to take everything in.

Zandia was the only known planet in the Universe to have exponentially thrived over time. History had shown how the nation's leaders and society as a whole had always worked hard to ensure the natural balance of their ecosystem was maintained. They'd found their way to coexist, causing no lasting damage to their world. Flora and fauna ran rampant and were encouraged to flourish. Structures were not hard or heavy in their space, instead they were light and airy, blending in with the surroundings, as well as working with the environment rather than against it.

The transporter was no different, and would allow her to make a gradual transition into the Zandian way of life.

"Would you like a tour of the public rooms before I show you to our space?"

"Yes, yes, I think I would." As they stepped off the gangway and onto the ship, moving through a grand entrance and into a large open space, he heard her inhale sharply and she reached up to hold his hand resting on her shoulder. It was something he was used to, the grandness of the official Zandian transporter, but in her seeing it for the first time, he saw it through fresh eyes.

Every person who walked into the grand meeting room, located on the topmost level of the ship, was awed by the sense of floating out amongst the galaxy. The way the room was designed showcased the ceiling, constructed entirely of a superior and unusual steel, of which also happened to be a major trading product for Zandia. They manipulated the raw ingredients, added in minerals that strengthened it further and then another set of materials were brought in during the heating phase. What resulted was a product of super strong steel, entirely see-through from the inside, and opaque from outside.

The ship housed approximately three hundred people. With staff to drive and maintain the ship, hospitality people, sex aides, the Zandian national speedball team, Xer's security staff, and more, it was a thriving hive of activity. The trip to Earth had been leisurely, with a couple of diplomatic stops made along the way, which they wouldn't be making on the return journey.

Xer and Sui walked to the side of the large greeting hall where a bank of tubes were located. He could tell she still wasn't used to the attention she drew as the Royal Heiress Apprentice. Although he thought the blush gracing her cheeks from all the stares her hair received was adorable.

"People seem intrigued by your lovely blonde locks. It won't be long before there is a call for the water authority to stop the supplements."

"I do seem to be attracting some interesting looks."

They stepped into a secured tube and viewed what all the other levels offered. He explained how there were some restricted floors but they were all opened to her. They visited each floor's public spaces first. The ones she seemed to have the most interest in were those dedicated to entertainment and eating. It was where the majority of people not working congregated, giving her a little snippet of home.

The last levels they visited had "restricted" listed on the directory in the tube but nothing else to denote what or where they were. After accessing these floors with retinal eye scan, they exited onto a secured level. Very quickly it became obvious why these areas were tightly protected and separated from the rest of the ship. The ship was fully armed and held its own force, separate from Xer's own security team. Once she'd been introduced to the General and his officers, they moved down to another floor of the ship where the navigation compartment was located. Sui was introduced to the transporters Marshal and Vice Marshal, and both expressed their honor at being the team to take the Royal Heiress Apprentice back to Zandia.

"Well?"

"It's an awful lot to take in, Xer, I know I'll get lost."

"No, you won't. Remember, you have your guards. They know the ship's layout. And, don't forget, you're never truly alone, I'm here."

"I forget how open Zandian society truly is, even how accessible the ruling clan is. On Earth, the leaders are rarely seen in person and if they are it's from behind armed walls."

"Are you afraid someone might harm you?"

"Actually I'm not. Although I have to say, since we boarded the ship, my excitement in going home has been growing."

Because he knew what the last unlisted floor was, once the tube pinged its arrival, Xer stepped back and motioned for her to walk before him. This was the level the royal residences were found, and he was nervous. Racing through his mind was a worry she might reject the first thing to truly reflect him and his personality.

The marble hallway, dotted with panels up and down the length, each guarded by a member of his personal security team, was quiet compared to every other floor they'd visited. They went through a double paneled entry and he heard her gasp. He was a big man and thus chose to surround himself with things large enough to accommodate him comfortably. But this space was more than the size of the items, it was a place in which he spent most of his time. He hoped his mate would feel the same sense of comfort and welcome.

One whole wall was open to the galaxy beyond. It was an inspiring view and one he never tired of enjoying. To the left sat his pride and joy—one entire end of the room covered from floor to ceiling in books. He enjoyed a variety of subjects, trying new ones all the time and delving fully into the subject, absorbing as much knowledge as he could. There were two large chairs and a double desk, waiting to be used. He rubbed his bald head in a moment of unease when he noticed she'd found his section of historical erotic art books. When she looked over her shoulder at him, he laughed.

"A man needs inspiration when he's traveling alone."

"Well, at some point during our trip, we'll have to look at these together. I'd like to see what turns you on."

"You turn me on, my sweet petite."

Xer watched as she moved toward the main function of the room. Sitting in the center of the thickly piled black carpet covering the floor was his bed, a totally unique piece of furniture he'd commissioned for this ship. A post at each of the four was the basic form, and the only thing simple about it. The bed, a grand fifteen foot high, was hand carved of black ebony wood and resembled the treetops in Zandia's Great Forest, with the mattress resting beneath their leaves.

He leaned back against the closed panels and watched as she walked up to the huge bed and rubbed her hands over the soft mossy green covering. His body responded to her seductive movements as if she'd been stroking him. Xer noticed the bed itself came up to her hips and made a mental note to contact the artisan who created the piece for a step stool for her to use.

"This room," she turned to him and glowed, "is very sumptuous."

"Through the panel over there," he pointed to his right, "is the wet room. And next to it is our dressing room. If there's anything missing, let me know and I'll see you get it." He was happy to see her in his space. This woman was his path-mate, and there was no doubt in his mind they were a perfect match.

"It's all too much to take in."

"I know it is, love, everything will be fine."

"Yes, I believe it will. Eventually."

Xer moved forward, pulled her into his arms and held her close. He gave her the comfort and security of his body.

"Love me, Xer?"

"I do."

"Here, now, make love with me on this bed of dreams."

"Oh, my precious, always and forever." He lifted her and laid her out in the center of the bed, beneath the dark boughs where their passion reigned.

Chapter Eighteen

Xer sat at his desk as they prepared to land on Zandia. He was surprised at how quickly time seemed to have passed while on the transporter with his mate for their voyage back home. They'd taken the time to get to know each other even better, deepening the bond they'd already built on Earth.

After they met with a mating advisor via a link, a formality to ensure the Royal Heir Apprentice had claimed a true path-mate, it was further determined he and Sui were heart-souls. This was a very rare coming together of two people who were the keepers of each other's heart and soul. This type of relationship meant they were true to each other and no other physical or emotional connections could be entered without causing serious harm to the other.

On Zandia, to find one's heart-soul was an exceptional occurrence, and something envied and celebrated by all. After a few discussions with his parents, it was decided they'd hold the binding ceremony shortly after their arrival. In fact, the rite had already been arranged and the entire planet was readying itself to celebrate. It was always a joyful day when a transporter arrived safely, but it was also a time to rejoice the national team maintaining the Speedball Champions of the Universe title, and even more importantly, their prince was about to join the rare group of people who'd found their heart-soul.

The binding ceremony was a set of formal rites in which the couple was required to share their joy and love with everyone. The advisor they spoke with would be the Master of Rituals who officiated over the event. Once the vows had been spoken, Xer, with the help of his chosen best man, would bind Sui to a sturdy frame however he wished and was to bring her to climax for everyone to witness.

But everything was about to change in more ways than anyone would've expected. The last link with his parents had thrown him for a loop and he wasn't entirely sure how to broach the subject with his mate. Sitting back in the large comfortable seat, one particular conversation they'd had came to mind and he made mental notes of the points she'd brought up in order to help him approach the latest news with her.

He remembered it well. It had taken place their first evening on board the transporter and the journey back to Zandia had already begun when they'd moved the chairs to sit before the wall open to the galaxy. It was an inspiring and wondrous sight to behold, but the first time he'd sat there with Sui at his side had been made even more special when she made herself vulnerable to him. She opened herself, heart and soul, to him.

For almost a full hour, they'd sat there lost in their thoughts. She'd started quietly speaking, almost as if thinking out loud, of how she saw life for women on Zandia.

"She should be free to choose how she wants to live, not how some group of men who don't know her decide after reviewing results from tests taken over many years. They are human beings who should be allowed to have some say in what they see for their future. Yes, a mature person, with specific details about their choices would be better equipped to make such major decisions. That way, if they enjoy the option of being a sexual aide, it's an informed pathline for them."

174

"What pathline would you have chosen for yourself?"

"The problem is this, while I was on Zandia, I saw no other opportunities, and once on Earth, there were so many I found interesting. I was very pleased with my translator's post I found. You and our connection to each other are very important to my emotional happiness, but I need more to feel like I'm living for myself. I believe it's imperative that I'm happy and fulfilled in order for me to be a complete and better partner in our life together." She'd been quiet for a few minutes before she finished.

"I learned quite a bit from my translation work. It's sad to admit this, Xer, but I was educated more about my home planet and how it works by looking at how strangers and other people approached Zandia than when I lived there. I wish I hadn't felt so in the dark about where I came from. Unfortunately it didn't take me long to realize it was because of my gender the information was withheld. It hurt and made me feel an outsider. The knowledge led me to believe I'd made the only choice for me. Nobody should ever be put in such a dangerous position."

Because he'd needed to feel her, as well as her acceptance of his support, he'd stretched out a hand and waited for her to clasp hold of his. He'd been taken aback by what she'd said that night, still was. Sui had felt like she wasn't a part of her home planet because of how she'd been treated, and sad as it was to say, she was most likely not the only one to feel this way. Maybe there'd been others who had left and hadn't been lucky enough to survive.

The confession had happened spontaneously, he'd not been able to bring up his anger shields, which before had allowed him to see no further than her being on Earth. Instead she'd laid it out there and he'd truly heard how desperate she'd felt about her problem on Zandia.

The peaceful moment ended as soon as the image of her alone on the other planet flashed across his thoughts. There were a few things he wasn't looking forward to doing upon returning home, one being meeting Ambassador Seccus, Sui's father. Normally Xer saw himself as an even-tempered man, but this was the one thing, no matter how much time passed, he hadn't been able to find stable footing with. His mate could have died or been seriously harmed by being left alone on a foreign planet. In more reasonable moments, he was able to see why the man did what he had for his daughter, but still his heart couldn't be brought into line with his brain on this. The only positive he was able to see in the situation was how it had enabled him to meet his only heart-soul mate.

Xer shook his head to shift the negativity away and stood, pacing his office like a caged animal. It was about time Zandia moved with the time and toward equality for all its citizens. He stopped in the middle of the room when the panel slid open.

"Hi, Stud! Let's celebrate. I just had my final fitting—what is it, what's the matter?"

"Hello, my sweet petite."

"Xer, what is it? You look fit to be tied."

She had such a calming affect on him. The minute her small hand laid across his forearm, he was done with his anger. But it was also an opportunity to tell her the news before someone else did.

"Everything's fine. Come, sit with me for a minute then we can talk. But first, tell me about your binding ceremony attire."

"You're trying to divert my attention and it won't work. Why were you upset when I walked in?"

Sighing deeply, all he could do was give her his honesty. "I was remembering how I found you living on Earth, alone, but you're here with me so it was wasted energy. Now, tell me about

176

what you're going to wear, standing on the platform before all of Zandia."

"Humph, no, you get no hints. You'll have to be surprised along with everyone else."

"I'll eagerly wait to see what sort of delicious confection you chose to enflame my already raging lust."

Sui settled on his lap, wiggled about, and he could think of nothing more than to sit back and enjoy her presence. He leaned down and nuzzled his nose into her curls then took a nibble from the sweet spot on her neck before she nudged him back.

"You know, I wouldn't change a thing if it meant I'd be sitting here with you as a claimed path-mate, about to be formally bound with you as my one heart-soul."

He took a deep breath before he spoke. "What would you say if on the day we went one step further?"

"What other official procedure is there but the one that binds us together for eternity?"

Xer looked into her eyes as he told her. "My parents, well, my father really, would like to take this opportunity to resign the crown and sword."

"No!"

"Why?"

"It's too soon! I don't know what to do! What if everyone hates me? No, Xer, no!"

"Listen Sui, we're the future. An example of what's possible for Zandians, women in particular."

"They'll hate me and you by default for bringing me back and changing everything they're comfortable with."

"No, I don't think so. I spoke with my father at length about some of the points you've brought up in regards to new pathlines being opened to women and he agreed with you. Because of what we're stating with our vows, he figures this next step is obvious and why delay it. Of course some of the things you and I would like to change aren't going to be agreeable to every person, it would be unrealistic to believe otherwise. But I think the choices open to the women aren't in keeping with where Zandia is headed, not if we want to truly be a world power."

"Oh dear, Xer, I wasn't thinking about anything other than how it would affect me, and not how this was the position you've been working to be ready for when this honor was bestowed on you. I mean, I was, but not in terms of reality, nor what was around the corner for our homeland. Suddenly it doesn't feel like the future is very many years away."

"I know, but Sui, this is what I see when I look at you. Besides being utterly beautiful, enchanting and my life partner, I see a modern woman who is self-sufficient, strong and intelligent. I know you'll make a wonderful and compassionate queen, a true role model for the people, particularly our young ladies with their entire lives before them. To help guide these women safely forward."

"See, this is why you should be king. You speak well, are a smart man—"

"Trust me."

He knew he had her when she finally laid her head on his shoulder and sighed.

"I do."

"Good. You'll see, everything will be fine."

"Does anything worry you?"

"Yes, you."

"I love you."

"You know what this means?"

"What?"

"Another set of ceremonial traditions we have to memorize?"

"Oh nuts!"

"And—"

"Don't say it!"

"Fittings."

"You don't have to have such a big smile on your face just because you don't have to go through it. All the poking and prodding gets tiring after awhile, no matter how beautiful the garment they produce. Oh, by the way, I now possess my first traditional Zandian chain mail garment."

"Really?"

"Yes, I should have a couple more by the time we land tomorrow."

"You know, I've wondered, do you still have the Six Turns to Love dress you wore the night I marked you? Now that was a garment you should wear more often."

His dick was getting hard, letting her know exactly how well he remembered their first evening together.

CB&CD

Two days later, Xer was back in his home but he wasn't settled. He felt empty without Sui at his side. The Ambassador was expected to arrive at any moment and Xer was working hard to maintain his calm. It was a meeting he'd requested, all in a bid for him to move beyond his anger. Before he could do anything, he needed to hear from the man himself how he'd been able to leave his daughter alone on a foreign planet.

Purposefully he turned his thoughts back to the beautiful woman who was his mate and couldn't hold back the pleasure racing through him. They'd bucked tradition and she'd stayed at his side yesterday so they could both enjoy the party celebrating Zandians maintaining the Speedball Champions of the Universe title. It was also an opportunity for the mates and folds of his team members to meet the woman who would be their future queen. They all appeared honored and pleased to be in her presence. He'd had no doubt but it was good for her to experience it all herself to truly believe.

He'd been rather pleased with himself and the smile that spreading across his face had been a sign he was very aware of it too. As predicted, he'd heard a group of ladies talking about her lovely blonde curls and how they too wanted hair as well. He'd expected it but Sui merely blushed when he told her. The future was looking good.

Unfortunately, everything wasn't perfect. As soon as the party had ended, he'd taken his mate back to the apartment his parents maintained for him in the palace and left her there. Officially they weren't supposed to spend any time together until they were bound. Thankfully Rol had delivered a secured link to her, allowing them to be able to speak whenever they wanted.

A soft bell rang and interrupted thoughts of his mate. Without moving a muscle, he switched from being a happy pre-bound man to a large tense warrior ready to face the world to protect his woman. Once his assistant dinged to announce the arrival of Ambassador Seccus, he strove for a more relaxed equilibrium.

He walked over to the panel, ready to greet the older man he'd briefly met before, but had had no other dealings with.

"Sir, a pleasure to meet you again."

"Ambassador. Please, have a seat." Xer waved a hand toward a chair resting before his desk as he moved around to sit behind the large and imposing piece. He folded his hands and made to get this over with. When he looked over and really saw the older man, he noticed he had his mate's blue eyes and all his well laid plans were lost.

"How could you leave your young daughter all by herself on a foreign planet?"

"Sir, I was there for some time before I was called away. I ensured she was settled in a job and home before I left."

"You think nothing else was necessary to see to her protection?"

"No, sir, I didn't, but it's all she'd allow me to do. What she has remained unaware of was the security team I'd hired to see to her everyday safety."

"What? I never saw anybody standing by to protect her."

"Two lived next door to her as a couple, another was housed on her floor at work as a Pelokian translator and the other had recently quit and a replacement had yet to be hired when she'd volunteered to be the translator for Zandia at the speedball competition. Sui'd surprised me. I hadn't expected her to put herself in a position of possibly being recognized. Either way, once they saw you and your team there, they stood down."

Xer shook his head. He was surprised he hadn't noted the local security, even if they had backed off. What did surprise him was how after all that time had passed and how careful she'd been, Sui hadn't noticed them either. He found the force had been taken out of his fury.

"Ambassador, I find that although I'm still upset, it's no longer worth the time or energy it takes to keep it spinning in my mind. Your daughter makes me very happy. I love her dearly, as she does me, and we both hope you and your fold will be a part of ours."

"Sir, there was never any doubt of our supporting your union. You know by now how very stubborn she is, and should understand the main reason I didn't send her back to Zandia was because I believed wholly in her need for a more fulfilling life."

"Well, as you're about to become part of my clan, I feel it's appropriate to fill you in on a few changes about to happen here on Zandia. They're to go no further than this room, of course."

"Of course, sir."

"Please, call me Xer, we're fold members now."

"Xer, and please, I am Ero."

Chapter Nineteen

Nervous energy raced through her body. She held up her hand and noticed how it shook wildly. She was terrified of how far her life had moved out of her control in such a short span of time. In less than an hour, she'd walk through that panel and enter a full day of events, her binding ceremony and now another rite, which also happens to be vitally important to the future of Zandia and the Universe. It was all so much to take in.

What if she messed up?

The first half of the day was going to be a dream. Being officially bound to Xer was sure to be the happiest moment in her life. She was eager to feel his supple ribbons securely wrapped around her wrists and ankles, holding her firmly in place for their pleasure. They hadn't spent a single minute in the past three days naked and enjoying each other's bodies as they had been since the moment they'd met. It left her existing in a state of eager anticipation of what was to come.

There'd been many meetings attended and preparations made, but by the end of each day, she'd been left a withering mass of need and desire, without a means of fulfillment other than the presence of her marked and claimed pieces. Her only saving grace was their being a heart-soul couple. She smiled, knowing Xer was also going through the same vow of abstinence. It'd been an easy decision for them to make, neither wanted another involved in their loving, although they weren't opposed to watching or being watched. They'd agreed sex was a healthy expression of an emotional connection between two people and why deny the pleasure to others.

Sui was looking forward to all of it, but the part following the binding ceremony, when they were enthroned, was what caused her a great deal of anxiety.

Once she'd been settled in Xer's apartment in the palace, the Roiroirepus clan's official jeweler had arrived and a queen's crown had been built around her head. The piece, one to match her mates, was constructed of carved onyx to resemble a branch of oak leaves. There were uncut aquamarine stones and black diamonds around the leaves, and fresh black pearls and moonstones dripping from the edges like water drops.

The Surian seamstress assigned to fashion her royal robe arrived and with the jeweler started to create a stunning garment for her to wear. They used the traditional sheer, black silk chiffon robe with a hood, then added a wide border of very fine onyx and aquamarine to form the Roiroirepus motto, "Forever Free". Mixed within this were and various symbols found in nature and representing Zandia's focus. The garment was one fit for royalty, stunning and elegant. The craftspeople had outdone themselves on her behalf.

After the jeweler and seamstress, and all of their assistants, had helped her dress left, she found the quiet soothing. It was all too much to take in, but she wouldn't think about any of it right then. She'd be fine once Xer was at her side.

A soft tap on the panel interrupted her musings.

"Yes?"

"May I come in, daughter?"

"Yes, of course, ma'am." She walked forward to greet her mate's mother, and was stopped from moving to her knees in formal greeting.

"No, there's no need for such formality between us. We're a part of the same fold, call me Tighia. Besides I don't want you to ruin your beautiful garment. You look simply stunning, Sui. I have no doubt my son will have great joy in binding you to him."

She felt sexy and knew Xer was going to want her to wear this garment again. In fact, she wouldn't be surprised if he wanted her to wear the shoes alone, they were that erotic. High-heeled black boots laced tightly up the back of her legs and ended around the middle of her thigh. The only other thing she wore was a soft aquamarine rubber corset, which delicately cupped her bare breasts and hugged her curves, until it ended on the outward curve of her hips. From the back of the garment dripped a multitude of black, wide ribbons of rubber, trailing on the floor behind her.

Mini-cups held her large breasts in a presentation position. The onyx shields covered her red nipples but there was no hiding the excited tips. They were always in a state of arousal with the aquamarine stones dancing at the end of the chains circling the disks, constantly whipping at her flesh. Nothing covered the blonde tuft of hair that decorated her pussy other than the mark hooked onto her hard clit and dripping between her thighs to end with the onyx bullet buried in her back rosette.

Since the day her marked and claimed jewelry had been placed on her body by Xer, she'd worn them proudly. She was eager and already begging for his loving attention.

"Thank you. I still can't believe all of this is happening to me. It feels like a dream or even someone else's happiness I'm watching." She was pleased to have such an easy relationship with her mate's parents. They were both very nice and seemed to genuinely be happy with their son's chosen mate.

"I wanted you to know, we couldn't be more pleased about how you and our son have chosen to accept the crown and sword of Zandia on this day. It was never a role we held comfortably and feel very strongly you and Xer are the future and will bring our world into a new time." The older woman held both Sui's hands and with her softly spoken words helped Sui find the confidence she needed to walk out of the room, and to her mate.

"Tighia, I'm grateful you took the time to come and give me these words. They are exactly what I needed to hear."

"You're most welcome. Now, I'm going to go and find my Rore. Oh, here is a note from my son, for your eyes only, he said." She smiled and handed over the little slip of paper before moving toward the panel. Before she left, the older woman offered one last statement. "Daughter, we wait for whenever you're ready."

Nodding her head, she waited until the other woman had left before opening the missive. It was simple and to the point. *You are my heart-soul, come to me now.*

Sui walked out of the dressing room, kissed the slip of paper, slid it beneath her pillow and left the private sanctuary. Outside the room, waiting to escort her to the theater, were the guards who'd been assigned to her back on Earth. She was thankful for the familiar faces and smiled at each of them before they walked forward.

There was no one to meet her at the panel, no one to deliver her into her mate's care. The movement away from some traditions was sure to cause a few shocked looks, but it was their way of making sure everyone understood they saw their union as a partnership, not an ownership. She'd spoken at length with her father about their choices, and how it wasn't meant as an insult to him, it was an expression of their relationship. She knew there was still some tension between the two men in her life, but figured in time it would settle down.

Using her own hands, she pressed open the large panels and stepped into the grand, open-air National Theater.

Instantly her gaze connected with Xer's, and she found the last boost of confidence she needed to walk easily down the aisle to him. Each step she made on the highly polished black marble floor echoed in the silence around her. Although she never took her eyes off her mate, she could sense the true mass of humanity who'd come to witness the binding ceremony.

She heard gasps as people noticed she walked alone, and the occasional comment spoken quietly about her hair. Her mate had been right, it was all the rage. All she saw was her lover standing tall and strong, in nothing but a pair of drawstring silk trousers, which looked to be barely hanging on to his hips. Sui worked hard to hold back the excited giggle threatening to burst forth, even from here she could see his impressive hard-on poking against the light fabric.

This binding ceremony was going to be fun.

Slowly she made her way forward but as was always the case, her marked and claimed pieces made it impossible to ignore her body's cravings. Already her upper thighs were damp with the honey she created and her nipples hardened further under the attention Xer focused on her. Sui basked in the warmth of his love.

As she made her way up a dozen or so stairs to the top of the platform, she was panting. Xer reached out a hand and helped her up the last couple steps until she stood in front of him.

"Finally you're here."

"I had to make sure I looked good for you."

"Little one, you're always stunning, and today, on our binding day, you are incomparable!"

"Prince Xer, sir? Ma'am? Are you ready?"

"Oh dear, um, sorry."

"We apologize, sir."

"Shall I begin?"

"Yes, please. We're ready, aren't we, Sui?"

"Definitely."

"Okay, please hold hands and face each other." The Master of Rituals waited until they were in place before he faced the crowd. "King Rore, Queen Tighia, ladies and gentlemen. We are gathered here today to witness the official binding of Sui of the Seccus Clan to Xer Rieh of the Roiroirepus Clan, Royal Heir Apprentice, Prince Xer III. This is the point where we break from tradition."

The crowd started talking amongst themselves, but Sui heard none of it and grinned at her mate.

"They haven't heard anything yet, have they, little one?" Only she heard his whispered aside and was hard-pressed to hold back the giggles still threatening to surface.

"Please, please, everyone," the Master's voice rose to be heard over the audiences chatter. "The heart-soul couple has written their own vows."

He walked over, stopped at their side, and advised Xer to begin, assuring him the witnesses would quiet down once they started to speak.

"I, Xer Rieh of the Roiroirepus Clan, have marked, claimed and now bind Sui Seccus, my heart-soul, to me for eternity."

"I, Sui Seccus, will now bind Xer Rieh, my heart-soul, to me for eternity."

Her simple vow was all it took to send the crowd wild. When he said her full name and she spoke her vow, something never done before, everyone on Zandia realized changes were coming. They smiled at each other and the real formalities began.

The Master clapped his hands and a large sturdy frame was sent up from beneath the platform, and sat ready for her to be strapped to it for their pleasure.

With a naughty smile, he led her to stand beneath the steel apparatus.

"Ready?"

"Always."

"Your hand, my love." He reached behind her and detached a ribbon from the back of her corset, wrapped it around her wrist, and tied it off, leaving the remainder streaming down. Xer did the same to her other wrist, before he kneeled, repeated the process with each ankle and two more were secured around her thighs.

She was quivering with excitement and knew he could see how turned on she was when he licked the moisture painting her upper thigh.

There were cameras all around the theater, covering the ceremony for those who weren't inside, but she saw none of them. Right then her world was Xer.

Using the black ribbons, he secured her arms up above her head. Sui felt no discomfort, only safety and happiness in his care. He nodded to someone behind her and to the side. She looked over her shoulder and saw Rol, his best friend and second-in-command, moving forward.

"You look beautiful, Sui."

"Thank you Rol."

With his hands on her ass and upper thighs, he lifted her up and held her steady while Xer used the strands around her thighs to tie her legs up and the ones around her ankles to secure them to the side so she remained spread open. She began to pant, feeling vulnerable now that all her limbs were fixed to the frame, ready for him to take her.

Any moment her heart was going to leap out of her chest. She looked up at her mate, standing between her legs, and was immediately relaxed by his calm demeanor.

"Shhh, it's all right, baby girl." As he spoke with her, he used a big finger to tease the lips surrounding the entrance to her pussy. Her body jumped in the ribbons. "You're wound tightly today, aren't you?"

"Oh yes, this abstinence thing has been horrible. I need you very much."

"I'm eager for you as well." He stepped closer and nudged her slit with his silk-covered hard-on. "No, we're eager for you, but there are a few formalities we must see to first." While he bumped against her cleft, he reached down and played with the onyx bullet in her ass, shifting it in and out.

Chapter Twenty

Xer took in his mate's secured limbs then looked down at her small blonde pelt and suddenly they were alone. The masses, cameras and formalities were forgotten, it was them loving each other and nothing else. Neither of them had any qualms about physically expressing themselves before others, because in the end, it was about them alone.

He reached up and strummed his thumbs over both her bright red nipple points, exposed and framed perfectly by the claiming disks. A deep moan erupted from between her lips.

"Oh you're ripe, ready to burst, aren't you?"

"Yes, yes I am. Please don't torment me this way. I'm ready. Thrust your hard cock inside me now. I know you're hard. I can see it, feel it, and I want it!"

"Don't worry, I will, but first I need to make you scream your pleasure."

"Xer?"

The future king kneeling down before anyone in public was not done, but as he did just that between Sui's legs, the witnesses rumbled with surprise. Smiling, he took two fingers and spread her dewed lower lips open. He used his thumb, wrapped it in a bit of his mark's remaining jeweled length draped between her legs, and eased it into her slit.

"Ohhh."

Each moan she released he felt in his dick, causing it to bounce with the need to bury itself inside her heat. Since they were forced to remain apart, he'd worn the cock ring she'd given to him rather memorably the night they won the speedball championship. It seemed only fair because the onyx band kept him hard and eager to ride once again between her legs, much as his mark and claiming pieces did for her. He stroked his other hand along her soft thigh exposed above her boot, around and over her ass, where he once again worked the onyx bullet in and out of her clenching rose.

"Oh-ohhh!"

Music to his ears but he needed more than to watch her splinter apart. Stretching forward, he danced the tip of his tongue across her exposed nub.

"Yes! Xer!"

"Mmmm, you're on edge, little one."

"Please, oh yes, more!"

"More what? More of this?" He increased the speed plunging the bullet in and out of her tight rose and he nibbled on her clit.

"Yes!"

"Or this?" Xer was enjoying watching her fall apart as he twirled his thumb around her opening, but not going in any further.

"Ohhh!"

She splintered when he used his front two teeth to bite onto her clit and tug.

"Ahhh! Xer!"

The need to taste her honey could no longer be denied. He thrust his tongue into her quaking depths and pulled out a taste to savor. Her passion was addictive and he sent his tongue in over and over again, looking for more of her juice as she continued to scream his name and other sexual demands.

"Take me, take me, take me." She chanted her need over and over.

He felt each word, every gasp she made and could no longer hold back his desperate need to plunge his hard-on into her hot, wet pussy.

Abruptly he stood and smiled over her screaming disappointment at a climax delayed.

"No!"

"Yes!" He stepped back and stripped off his pants, taking in how beautiful his mate appeared all strung up and panting with pleasure. Her mouth was parted and lids were lowered, covering her blue eyes, but he knew she could see him. Xer held his cock in his hand and stroked it with purpose and it didn't take long.

"That's mine! Now bring your bejeweled rod over here and fuck me!"

"Whose?"

"*Mine!*"

"It certainly is, baby girl." He moved in between her legs, close enough to feel her soft inner thighs against his hips. Lodging the crown in her heat, he pushed in a small length to tease her further. "Here you go, here it is, all at once."

"Uhhh!"

Hard, without pause, he thrust until he bottomed out in her pussy. His balls pressed against her ass and the rings dangling chunks of aquamarine pressed into her eager flesh. Even with the ring on, Xer knew he wouldn't last long. His mark, along with the cock ring he wore, further stimulated the length of his dick as he plunged in and out of her silken grip.

Now his control was being tested further as her moist walls continually clenched around him.

Sliding out until only the crown remained, he watched as she tensed her legs, fighting against the restraints holding her captive for him. He could no longer fight his more base instincts to thrust hard and fast, over and over again, until she was a writhing mass of nerves dangling from his ribbons.

"Here!" With all the power he possessed, he gave everything in him, body and soul, to his beloved. He pushed into her tight clench, carving a space for himself. Looking down, he saw his big hands firmly holding on to her hips and hoped they were giving her a sense of security in his loving. But his gaze kept drifting to where they met, the place where they were beyond touching, but fully connected, and Xer knew it was an image forever etched on his brain.

"I'm almost there!"

"Ungh! So tight, and your big tits are bouncing, begging me for attention." There was no way he could deny their call a moment longer. Slowing down the thrusting brought a moan bubbling up and slipping out from between her lips. The moment his hands were up and teasing the red tips with his strumming thumbs, he went back to moving his cock in and out of her grip.

"Ohhh, please give me more, fuck me!"

He loved to hear her plead, because he'd do anything to give her whatever she wanted and this he could do with ease. Using his thumbs and first fingers, he pinched her nipples, hard, and used his grip to hold her steady as he began shafting her.

"Xer!"

Each plunge harder and faster than the last, he took everything she offered and yelled with triumph as she once again fell apart.

"Ahhh! My woman!"

Everything was different the moment Sui opened her eyes and looked up at him. Her light blue orbs were full of love and desire, and when his gaze trailed down to her full red lips, he bowed before their message.

"I forever love you."

"Argh!" As impossible as it seemed, his cock grew harder, and a copious amount of seed shot from the depths of his soul as he tried to tell her coherently how he loved her, but instead it came out on a growl.

For a moment he luxuriated in their spent passion, but because of her position, he couldn't hold her close as he would've liked. Stepping back from his lover, he stumbled and Rol was there to hold him steady. So lost in each other, the simple touch brought him both back to their binding ceremony, and the reality there was still more that needed to be done before he could hold his mate as he preferred.

"Thanks, I forgot."

"It's all right, the witnesses have never seen the likes of you two before and are spellbound by the passion you two expound. It's old hat to me."

"Ha!" A little levity was all he needed to bring it back together, a good laugh with his friend was the perfect solution. "Will you help me?"

"With pleasure."

They both were struck silent by the beauty hanging limply before them, but Xer couldn't look beyond her sweet slit as it dripped his cum onto the platform.

"You truly are a lucky man. She'll be a wonderful mate for you and an ideal queen for Zandia. Now let's get this show on the road before everyone out there is too busy fucking to realize they have new leaders."

Rol went and stood behind Sui to hold her steady as Xer worked on untying the various rubber ribbons holding her suspended.

"You okay, sweet petite?"

"Oh my."

"I take it that's a yes." He laughed and held her hips as she gained her footing. Once he felt she was steady, he looked over at the Master of Rituals and nodded. Holding hands, they watched as the frame was sent down beneath the platform and Rol stepped away, leaving them to face the Master as an almost bound couple.

The binding ceremony was nearly finished and she felt ready to call it a day. She hadn't realized how much it would take out of her, being suspended as she and her mate shared their love for an entire world to witness.

Pleasure still ran rampant through her body, but it was feeling Xer's seed trailing down her thigh that held her attention. Sure there was a random thought spared for the beautiful boots but it was short-lived—they'd survive for another day.

Slowly her focus cleared and she looked out at all the people who were there to witness their binding. She was shocked she'd been able to forget they were there, watching her and her heart-soul bind themselves to each other. They looked stunned speechless, and she wasn't sure how to take it.

"Are you ready?" The Master of Rituals waited for them both to nod before he continued. "We have witnessed an incredible coming together of these two people who stand before us in their desire to be bound to each other, and only each other, for as long as they both shall live. Is there anybody here who does not think either of these two people are suited for the life of a bound couple?"

The silence was heavy and felt like it lasted forever. She had no worries, everyone must see how completely devoted they were to each other.

"Wonderful. Who does this couple trust with their binding cuffs?"

Rol stepped back onto the platform carrying a black box with carvings of two wild nimaks cavorting through nature. She looked up at him and found the second-in-command's smile infectious. It had been easy to choose him as their trust keeper. He'd been at their side through everything and she felt he had their best interests at heart.

"I, sir, Rol Tunociv, Commander of the Zandian TransFleet."

"Excellent. Xer Rieh, please take the left arm of your mate and place this cuff on her for all time while stating your rules."

"I am binding Sui Seccus to my side and promise—" The witnesses erupted with a gasp of surprise. Her mate smiled at her and countered by speaking even more loudly, "—to ensure she is safe, happy, healthy and leads a fulfilling life. I promise to be a father who participates in our children's upbringing. I promise to love and honor her for as long as we live and beyond."

By the time he spoke the last word, the theater was once again silent but Sui was focused on her man and the beautiful cuff he'd slid up her arm to rest above her bicep. It reminded her of their crowns, onyx carved to resemble a tree branch.

There was no discomfort or unease with its presence. In fact, the cuff felt like it had always been there and always would.

But now it was time for the biggest shock for the witnesses. Traditionally women were bound to the man and his rules, but they were binding themselves to each other and that meant she had rules to state as she placed a matching cuff on his arm.

"Sui Seccus, please take the left arm of your mate and place this cuff on him for all time while...um, stating your rules." The theater gasped as one, then just as suddenly, was eerily silent. Nobody walked out or called for a dispute, maybe King Rore was right and the time for change was here.

She lifted his arm and started the cuff's progress up his heavily muscled arm. Smiling, she kept her eyes on his and spoke her rules loud and clear.

"I am binding Xer Rieh to my side and promise to ensure he is happy, healthy and leads a fulfilling life. I promise to be a mother who cherishes any and all of the children we may be gifted with. I promise to be a wife and lover who will honor you for as long as we live, and beyond."

"King Rore, Queen Tighia, witnesses, please join me in congratulating our newly bound couple."

For a moment, it was silent, then a loud cheer broke out. The king and queen walked up onto the platform and offered their personal, and heartfelt, congratulations. Xer and Sui were hugged and kissed, hands were clasped and then the man who ruled the planet called for the attention of the witnesses and Sui's moment of calm passed. She reached out and grasped hold of her mate's hand for support, and felt Rol step up behind them.

"Great citizens of Zandia, your attention please." The theater went quiet and he made a brief but well thought out speech. "We could not have asked for a better heart-soul for our son than Sui. As you all know, it was a surprise to find myself leading Zandia, and every year since gaining the crown and sword, I did what I thought was best for the populace and planet."

The witnesses clapped and cheered. It was obvious they genuinely liked him.

"There was much I wanted to do but allowed myself to be persuaded to turn in another direction. Well, that will no longer happen. I officially resign in favor of my son Xer and his bound mate Sui."

And again, as one, the crowd let out a shocked gasp.

Chapter Twenty-One

It was absolute silence for what felt like an eternity surrounding them, but she knew there was no turning back now. Sui stood straight and sure beside her larger than life mate, ready to face whatever may happen next. She was surprised at how easily the citizens of Zandia had accepted her as the mate of their prince, knowing at some point she'd be queen. She supposed they hadn't expected it to happen this soon.

Shorter than she'd thought possible, she'd been accepted with open arms. Despite being short with a head full of curls, busty and curvaceous, and worse still, having lived alone on a foreign planet. No, she hadn't anticipated the welcome she'd received thus far. Even the cheer they'd received at her stating binding rules, a first for any woman on Zandia, had been a surprise.

Lost in her thoughts, it took a moment for her to realize the noise she was hearing wasn't a mirage but was actually happening right then. The witnesses were shouting, jumping up and down and trying to rush the stage.

"Are they going to lynch me?"

"No, my love, they're cheering."

"How can you tell?"

"There are no weapons pulled."

"Ah, yes, that would be a sign, wouldn't it?"

"Everything will be fine, my beloved heart-soul. Are you ready to be enthroned?"

"Oh crumb, this is going to happen."

"Yes, little one. Shall we?"

She took a deep breath and many thoughts rushed through her mind. After the next hour, she'd be the reigning queen of Zandia, no longer a single woman living on a strange planet working as a translator. Although she wasn't sure she knew how to handle the responsibility of being a role model for the modern Zandian woman, she was positive there was no other pathline for her to follow.

Nodding her head, Sui looked up at her heart-soul. "Ready."

Together they looked at King Rore and formally accepted the honor.

The witnesses had settled down some, but the theater was permeated with euphoria and the promise of a new future was welcomed with enthusiasm.

"Madame?"

It took a long moment to realize the Master of Rituals was speaking to her. Not only was she now a Madame, she was about to be Queen!

"Oh yes, sir?"

"Please, we need you to take off your binding garments, you need to come to your coronation completely bare."

"Yes, right, of course."

"Will someone please takes these back to our rooms, I'd like to keep them, maybe wear them for my mate some night."

"Certainly, Madame."

"Xer, will you help me?" Looking over her shoulder, she noticed how serious Xer appeared, and lifted a questioning eyebrow.

"You look utterly delicious in your binding attire." She felt his hand stroke over a butt cheek. "Do you promise to wear the boots for me later? Only the boots?"

"Definitely." Feeling strong and wicked, she gave a hip shimmy, which had the crowd roaring for more.

"You saucy woman." He started to work on unlacing her beautiful rubber garment with all the ribbons back in place, dripping along her back and spilling onto the floor. Rol stepped forward and waited for the items to be given to him. Sui didn't see but knew her mate went to his knees and unlaced the thigh high boots. Their trust companion held out his arm to hold her steady as she stepped out of the stupendous heels. Once he held all three pieces he left the platform with Rore and Tighia.

There was no embarrassment in standing nude before the people of their planet but her nerves were definitely mounting. She had just been through a binding ceremony and, it didn't matter it had been expected, being thrown straight into another traditional ritual was full of pressure and stress.

"It'll be okay, we're in this together."

The softly spoken words from her mate were all she'd needed. With a smile, she looked back at the Master and nodded.

"We've been granted a wonderful day to rejoice in the binding of Xer and Sui, and now we are entering another moment in history, one which will never be forgotten." The rite was briefly interrupted with a burst of clapping and cheers. After a few minutes, he called them all back to attention.

"Xer and Sui Rieh, do you swear to advocate and respect the needs of the Zandian people and planet?"

"Yes, I swear!" they answered in unison, sparking another explosion of happiness from the audience.

"Xer and Sui Rieh, do you swear to promote and encourage the advancement of the Zandian people and planet?"

"Yes, I swear!"

The witnesses again let their pleasure be known as the Master of Rituals leaned in to be heard and asked them to please join for the latter part of the formalities.

She faced her mate and smiled. "You ready?"

"For you, always." With hands on her hips, he lifted her up as she wrapped her legs around his hips. Reaching a hand down, she grasped hold of his hard, ringed cock and held it steady as she lowered herself onto him. There was no need for any further preparations. She was still in a high state of arousal and it was obvious by the strength of his hard dick he was as eager as she.

Once she was seated, Xer couldn't help himself from moving her petite form up and down his hard-on. He wanted to spend many an endless day like this, loving his heart-soul. It was no surprise he was ready for more and would most likely be on the verge of coming forever, but right now he had to maintain his composure.

"Uhhh!"

"Let them hear you sing, baby. Let them feel our pleasure." He started to bounce her, hard, on and off his cock. Not sure how he had the wherewithal but he looked to the side and there was Rol, ready to help as their trust companion. Nothing else was needed, the man knew them well. He stepped up behind Sui and softly asked her to move her arms from around her mate's neck. He assured her he was there behind her to ensure she didn't fall.

There was no doubt she'd lean back into their friend's safe hands, allowing him, and all the witnesses, to watch as he fucked their future queen. On and off his dick she moved. Xer would be forever entranced by the glory of her large breasts shaking before his very gaze.

"Ohhh, so much—uhhh, pleasure!"

"Right now everyone is watching us. They see our desire and want to immerse themselves in it. Let's share with them." He was struggling to hold on to his control. The enormity of the situation held no power over him, although he was aware of it. He wallowed deeply in his pool of passion and fought his urgent need to come in his mate's hot wet clenching pussy. He hoped he'd judged the timing correctly.

"Xer!"

"Yes, I'm right there with you!" Quickly he looked over and nodded to the Master. They were ready for the final pledge.

Knowing how crucial the timing was, the man hurried forward and shouted his last query.

"Xer and Sui Rieh, do you swear to bring support, growth, love and happiness to the Zandian people and planet?"

"Yes!" They came in unison as they pledged themselves to their world. There'd been little else he could do as the tight slit squeezed his throbbing cock over and over again. It'd been close, but nothing else mattered as his cum shot into her depths, and Xer knew everything would be all right.

He was thankful for Rol's help with moving his mate's arms back around his neck. With a satisfied smile on his face for all to see, he leaned back and caught the eye of his heart-soul and they declared together, "I swear."

The Master of Rituals called Rore and Tighia forward and each placed the carved onyx crowns atop the joined couple's heads, followed by Rol placing the heavier majestic robes over each of their shoulders.

"Rore and Tighia, witnesses, all the people of Zandia, please welcome King Xer and Queen Sui. May their reign be long and fruitful for all."

They were almost knocked over by vocal support sent their way. Laughing she climbed off him and, while holding hands and once again with his seed slipping down her thighs, they set about accepting all the joy and love being sent to them via the people of their planet.

Epilogue

Announcement from the Royal Court of Zandia

"The King and Queen of Zandia officially proclaim the pathline process will be restructured to ensure more options are open to the Zandian female.

"This planet will move forward into the future with the help of both men and women. Effective immediately for the current thirteenth year children, retesting will begin with the business and cross-Universe relations pathlines now open to females. The military line will be available after further consultations have been made.

"Testing parameters will be changed to reflect these amendments. Appointments at the educational facilities with qualified personnel will be made for every Zandian citizen to ensure they're aware of the other options now available. Changes will be made to pathlines where they are needed.

"No person, male or female, will be forced to live a pathline they feel is not their choice."

About the Author

To learn more about Tilly Greene, please visit www.tillygreene.com. Send an email to Tilly at tilly@tillygreene.com or join her Yahoo! group at http://groups.yahoo.com/group/tilly_greene to receive a copy of the Monthly Scorcher, new releases, contests and much more!

Look for these titles by
Tilly Greene

Now Available

New Beginnings: Carpe Diem

*How would you feel if you found out life, as you
know it, is all a lie?*

New Beginnings: Carpe Diem
© 2006 Tilly Greene

After the third world war, Earth is drastically damaged. By the twenty-third century, generations have passed, the facts twisted, history revised so it is unrecognizable and a utopian society is established below ground. Or is it?

Major Cooper Sayer, an imposing intelligent member of the special security forces, and Maris Gower, a peaceful soul who works in the New American Central Library, are an officially partnered couple. Life is comfortable, full of love for each other, and yet it took them less than fifteen minutes to decide on making a risky change.

With the dangers of residing below ground growing daily and the low life expectancy rate continually dropping, chances of a long and happy life together are becoming remote. The complete trust Maris has in Cooper is never questioned, even when he tells her they are going above for a chance at a longer life. A place that she has always believed meant instant death.

The adventure starts now.

Available now in ebook and print from Samhain Publishing.

Sacrilege. Mari was sure she was committing some crime somewhere, but there was no hope for it. The man before her inspired wicked thoughts. This was no pretty-boy Paris. No, this was a warrior in the truest sense of the word. And yet, at the same time, he was everything beautiful, strong and true, and perfect for her.

Six foot four inches of pure male excellence stood with his back to her, so Mari felt free to peruse the sight at her leisure and with pleasure. Both his arms were thrust up high on the doorjamb. He appeared to be enjoying whatever breeze came through the opened doorway, while he took in the view of the sea beyond. His head was thrown back, showing how his ruffled, chestnut brown hair hung down slightly longer than she knew he usually wore it, curling lightly around a crown of golden laurel leaves.

A slight sheen clung to his well-defined back and clearly showed he felt the heat of the day, despite its zenith having passed some time ago. His position, with more weight on one foot, shifted his bottom into a delicious pose and encouraged her lustful thoughts to bloom.

This was all wonderful, but the sight that had her holding her breath was found lower down. Lower, where the skirt defied gravity by barely hanging onto the top of his perfectly taut cheeks. She saw the start of his crease and a sexy little freckle slightly to the side. There was a waistband made from a stiffer fabric, with a carmine and gold meander pattern, before a more fluid fabric fell to mid-thigh with each side well slit. She guessed the openings were for ease of movement but personally felt it was more for a man's convenience.

The skirt's white silken fabric was soft and flowing, the edges fluttered in the breeze, but it still clung lovingly to his perfectly rounded, muscular ass. Her fingers itched to cup the firm cheeks gently before slowly moving around his waist to lay against his stomach. Or maybe she would use the vents to move her hands down between his legs to stroke his prime piece of personal steel, feel the hitch in his breath and know the exact moment she had his full attention.

Mari moved her gaze from the backside of the universe slowly down the lightly haired, heavily muscled legs to the brass guards covering his calves. But it was the heavy boots which caused her to frown. It brought to mind that, yes, Cooper was godlike in beauty and possessed many wonderful qualities and had cast a spell on her senses, but in his heart, he was all-warrior, the ultimate warrior.

Since Cooper had come into her life, she had enjoyed their time together, both in and out of bed, and now understood she had gone so far as to fall in love with him. At no time had she felt there could be a future for them beyond what they currently had, although she had definitely dreamed of them being a family, as husband and wife with kids, everything.

But happily ever after did not come her way.

Cooper had to tell her. He didn't think he'd been beating around the bush about how serious his feelings for her were, but then again, he hadn't come right out and said the words either. If he didn't tell Mari straight out that he loved her, he might lose her, and that was unacceptable.

How had his life reached this point? He was always in control, be it personally or professionally. Lives depended on it.

Although, at this moment in time, he didn't feel like he had full command of his life. He'd felt the wall she had put up from the start but thought he had reassured her, overcome any of her misconceptions and worries about tying herself to a man such as him. But lately he started to doubt she understood she was his.

Forever his.

He had done everything he could think of to show her how much she meant to him. Lately he'd been left with the impression she was waiting, for what he didn't know, but he would find out tonight and no later. He was not a patient man.

In fact, right now he was a hot man! Standing in the doorway with the sea before him, he hoped for any and all breezes available to come to him. Cooper wondered when his little sexy bit of everything would make an appearance, for he had some serious plans for her tonight. And it was not going to be the party she thought they were attending.

With a deep, gut level sigh, Cooper opened his eyes and looked out at the beach in front of him, thinking back to the moment he first saw his Mari.

It was minutes from sunset. He was naked and starting his dash down the sand to dive headfirst into the surf to cool off, both from the oppressive heat and the ineptness he'd seen over the past few days. Tonight his attendance was required at a dinner party. After that he would move on to enjoy an annual, bacchanal event with friends. If truth be told, he was not looking forward to either event.

A sharp noise to his right had him reaching for his weapon, only it wasn't there. He pulled to an abrupt stop. He could see her fairly well for being about twelve feet away, but had the impression she wasn't able to see him as clearly with the sun at his back.

Her long hair, hanging past her waist, was free and slightly mishandled by the wind. Her face was oval, with almond-shaped eyes and lips, slightly opened in a shocked "O" shape.

The details were foggy in this lighting and distance, but he easily discerned she was a tiny bit of something wonderful and most likely wouldn't reach his shoulders. Her beach attire, a length of fabric, wrapped around what appeared to be much more than a handful up top and curvy hips.

She giggled, placed a small delicate hand up to cover her mouth and started backing up, picking up her hem to keep from tripping. Before he could say more than a "hello", she turned and headed down the beach at a soft jog, sneaking peeks at him from over her shoulder.

He started to take off after her when he looked down and remembered he was nude, with his dick at full stand, and decided it best not to follow. He yelled "Come back, I won't hurt you," for good measure, but knew it wouldn't do much good when he heard the answering squeal of laughter. He didn't know how she found her way onto his private beach but he was going to have to keep an eye open for this little beauty.

Later, upon arriving at the dinner party in honor of the new doctor, Cooper instantly noticed the curvy blonde at the side of the room. With one look, he knew the shy, little thing standing against the wall was his siren from the beach. Before greeting his hostess and host, he marched right over, stood confidently between the room and her, and gently picked up her hand.

"I am Cooper Sayer, and I would very much like to know you better."

She gasped in reaction to his bold measures.

He knew his actions did not follow the usual path, nor it seemed, had anyone ever bucked society's rules in any way for her. He watched her intently as she anxiously looked around the room before lowering her eyes and quietly answered, "I am Mari..."

Cooper felt tiny hands gently rest on either side of his hips, above his skirt, feathering from his hipbones up his sides. With whispered reverence but delivered on a deeply felt groan, he breathed, "Mari." The name of his heart's desire floated out and he closed his eyes to savor the moment. She was very real, in his house, touching him, no longer a mere memory.

GET IT NOW

MyBookStoreAndMore.com

GREAT EBOOKS, GREAT DEALS . . . AND MORE!

Don't wait to run to the bookstore down the street, or
waste time shopping online at one of the "big boys." Now,
all your favorite Samhain authors are all in one place——at
MyBookStoreAndMore.com. Stop by today and discover
great deals on Samhain——and a whole lot more!

Samhain
Publishing, ltd

WWW.SAMHAINPUBLISHING.COM

Discover eBooks!

THE FASTEST WAY TO GET THE HOTTEST NAMES

Get your favorite authors on your favorite reader, long before they're out in print! Ebooks from Samhain go wherever you go, and work with whatever you carry—Palm, PDF, Mobi, and more.

WWW.SAMHAINPUBLISHING.COM

Printed in the United States
117118LV00002B/223-228/A